HIDING IN
PLAIN SIGHT

To Usman

Best wishes!

Valerie
Sherrard

A Shelby Belgarden Mystery

HIDING IN PLAIN SIGHT

Valerie Sherrard

A BOARDWALK BOOK
A MEMBER OF THE DUNDURN GROUP
TORONTO

Editor: Barry Jowett
Copy-editor: Jennifer Gallant
Design: Jennifer Scott
Printer: Webcom

National Library of Canada Cataloguing in Publication Data

Sherrard, Valerie
    Hiding in plain sight / Valerie Sherrard.

ISBN-10: 1-55002-546-5
ISBN-13: 978-1-55002-546-0

    I. Title.

PS8587.H3867H52 2005   jC813'.6   C2005-900170-4

1   2   3   4   5   09   08   07   06   05

  Conseil des Arts du Canada   Canada Council for the Arts   ONTARIO ARTS COUNCIL CONSEIL DES ARTS DE L'ONTARIO

We acknowledge the support of the **Canada Council for the Arts** and the **Ontario Arts Council** for our publishing program. We also acknowledge the financial support of the **Government of Canada** through the **Book Publishing Industry Development Program** and **The Association for the Export of Canadian Books**, and the **Government of Ontario** through the **Ontario Book Publishers Tax Credit** program, and the **Ontario Media Development Corporation's Ontario Book Initiative**.

Care has been taken to trace the ownership of copyright material used in this book. The author and the publisher welcome any information enabling them to rectify any references or credit in subsequent editions.

                                                                    J. Kirk Howard, President

Printed and bound in Canada.⊛
Printed on recycled paper.

www.dundurn.com

Dundurn Press   Gazelle Book Services Limited   Dundurn Press
8 Market Street, Suite 200   White Cross Mills   2250 Military Road
Toronto, Ontario, Canada   Hightown, Lancaster, England   Tonawanda, NY
M5E 1M6   LA1 4X5   U.S.A. 14150

This book is affectionately dedicated with love and thanks to my sixth grade teacher, Mr. Alf Lower, who planted the seed that grew.

CHAPTER ONE

It was a warm, sunny morning early in August — a perfect day to hang out with friends by the river or just goof off around town. In my case, though, I didn't have anywhere in particular to go. The house was empty when I got up, so I was kind of rattling around, antsy and in the mood to go somewhere.

A note in the kitchen told me that Dad was at work and Mom had gone off on some picture-taking excursion. She'd started off as a total amateur a few years back but she got some books and learned a lot about photography and developing pictures and all that stuff. Now, she sells some of her work to the local paper — mostly wildlife pictures or candid shots of townsfolk.

My boyfriend, Greg, was away with his dad, visiting relatives in Russell, Ontario. I'd never even heard of the place before Greg had told me they were going there, but

I'd discovered it was a little town near Ottawa. According to Greg, it was so small that it didn't even have a theatre.

My best friend, Betts, was away too. That was really aggravating, because the last time I'd talked to her she'd been pretty upset — so upset, in fact, that she couldn't even talk about it. I hadn't found out what was wrong before she left with her folks for summer vacation. They go away for a whole month, and there are still two weeks left, so I won't be able to find out what was bothering her until she gets back. If it was even something important enough that she remembers it, that is. Betts is kind of, well, inclined to overreact at times. It's perfectly possible that she'll have forgotten the whole thing by the time I see her again — after me worrying about it for the past few weeks.

Anyway, as I was saying, I really had nowhere to go, which was a thought that kept popping into my head as I laced up my runners. Still, I wasn't going to sit around the house all day. I'd been doing that for the last two weeks, on account of being grounded.

I'd rather not talk about that, though, since it seemed a bit harsh to me, considering that the trouble I'd been in had been for a good cause. My folks had actually agreed with me about that, but they had still insisted on giving me stiff consequences for it.

So, there it was, the first day I was allowed out, and I had nothing in particular to do. I thought maybe I'd just take a walk around, in case I happened to meet up with someone from school or whatever.

I headed across town, taking the route I normally use when I'm going to Greg's place. Instead of turning where I usually do, though, I kept on to the town square, where a cluster of stores form the perimeter of a park. The park has a few benches and a bunch of flowerbeds, with a big statue of some guy named Lord Beaverbrook in the middle. I don't know who he is, but there are a few buildings around here named for him, so he must have done something important at some point in history.

It briefly crossed my mind that I could go to the library and look up this Beaverbrook dude, but I dismissed it pretty fast. I guess it wouldn't hurt to know what was up with him and all, but this wasn't the day for it. It was too nice out, and I'd been trapped indoors for too long.

I avoided walking through the park itself, though that would have been the quickest route to the next street I was going to take. I'm sure the whole spot was designed to be a nice, peaceful place to sit when you're out shopping, but it sure isn't like that. There are always a few people hanging around the benches, but they're generally not the sort you'd want to park your grandmother beside if she needed to rest her feet for a bit.

Usually, it's mainly guys hanging around there. Most of them are in their twenties, but there are exceptions, and they range anywhere from a few years older than me to pretty old, like in their forties or even fifties.

It's not that they're actually doing anything wrong, at least not that you could see right off, but they've definitely taken over the park and now no one else uses it. The best I can explain it is that their presence creates a kind of atmosphere that doesn't exactly invite anyone else in.

As I skirted around it I got thinking about that and wondering what it was about these guys that so completely discourages anyone else from using the park. Was it accidental or something they did deliberately?

I know one thing — their appearance probably has a lot to do with it. Most of them look as though they've taken a pretty relaxed approach to personal hygiene, to the point that you'd have to wonder if they even had access to running water. Their clothes back up the apparent philosophy that cleanliness is highly overrated.

I was trying to decide if this was enough to ensure that others stayed away, or if there was more to it, when my attention was caught by the sound of a siren. In fact, it nearly made me jump out of my skin, the sudden blast screaming into the air on the next street over.

Naturally, I was curious. Who isn't, when they hear a siren?

The most annoying part for me is that I can't tell one emergency vehicle from another. I guess they must make different sounds, but I never know if I'm hearing a police car or an ambulance or a fire truck.

It seemed like a good idea to check it out, just to see if there was anything astir. My conscience tugged at me just the slightest bit because I'd more or less promised Greg that I'd steer clear of trouble while he was away. I dismissed that by telling myself *I* wasn't really interested, but that I should check it out for Betts. She loves to hear everything that's going on and she'd be so proud of me if I had a tidbit for her when she got back home.

I hurried along the street to the corner, where I quickly discovered that the source of this particular siren had been an ambulance.

I told myself *again* that I wasn't being nosy, though it was getting a bit hard to convince even myself. Then I sauntered casually in the direction the ambulance had taken. It came to a stop near a building that was familiar to me, which helped me persuade myself that I really *should* check out what was going on. Just in case it involved someone I knew or something.

It's kind of hard to look nonchalant when you join a crowd of people who are standing around waiting to see who happens to be sick — or, for that matter, dead. I mean, we all knew why we were there, yet we were all acting like our interest was somehow legitimate, instead of macabre, which is closer to the truth.

VALERIE SHERRARD

I swear, I never used to be the least bit interested in stuff like that. A year ago I'd have walked right past and never given it a thought. Lately, though, I seem to run into trouble on a regular basis, and I guess my outlook is changing because of that.

It seemed to take the ambulance attendants a long time to come back out. When they finally appeared, a stretcher rolled between them. With a start, I recognized its occupant as Howard Stanley, an octogenarian I'd met there recently when I was sort of doing an investigation. He was a sweet, helpful old guy, so it was alarming to see him grimacing in obvious pain as he was rolled toward the back of the ambulance.

I briefly considered going in to ask the landlady if she knew what was wrong with him, but she's not the sort you can get a sensible answer out of very easily. I abandoned that idea and decided I was going to have to mind my own business after all.

It's weird how bad I felt the rest of the day, thinking about poor Mr. Stanley. Having met him only once, it wasn't as though I knew him well or anything. Still, he'd been so nice. On top of that, I'd gotten the impression that he didn't have a lot of visitors. If I remember correctly, he has a daughter somewhere in town, but it seemed to me that he only saw her on Sundays. I suppose the rest of the week would be pretty long, all alone in an apartment.

12

That's when I remembered Ernie.

Mr. Stanley didn't live all alone after all — he had a cat. I pictured how the little thing had been curled in a ball on the floor while his owner and I chatted, and I got to worrying about who was going to take care of him while Mr. Stanley was in the hospital.

Probably his daughter would do it. But who knew for sure?

The next morning, still bothered by the thought of both the old guy and his cat, I decided it wouldn't hurt to pop over to the hospital to see him. That way, I could make sure he was okay and that someone was taking care of Ernie.

And I *wasn't* just being nosy. Honest!

CHAPTER TWO

A bored-looking lady at the reception desk typed Mr. Stanley's name into her computer and then told me his room number. Her voice was flat and she kind of looked past me while she gave me the information. I felt as though I'd inconvenienced her horribly somehow.

I thanked her anyway, or, I should say, I thanked the top of her head, since she was already bent forward again, looking at some papers spread out on the desk.

Mr. Stanley's room was on the second floor. When I emerged from the elevator, signs with arrows and numbers told me to go left. I followed the directions to his room, hesitating outside the door.

I'd met him only once before — he was sure to think it odd that I'd come to see him. He probably wouldn't even remember me. I nearly turned back, but

I just had to find out for sure that his cat, Ernie, was okay. I couldn't stand the thought of the poor little thing left alone, maybe starving.

The first thing that struck me when I walked into his room was how pale and shrunken he looked compared to the other time I'd seen him. I hoped my face didn't show the shock of seeing him like that. I guess if you're old and in the hospital, you'd just as soon not see people looking at you all horrified.

"Hello, Mr. Stanley?" I felt stupid at how that came out as a question. I *knew* who he was all right. There was no need to sound like I wasn't sure.

"Yes." He squinted a bit, like he was trying to get me in focus. "Well, this is a surprise. You're that girl, the one who came looking for her friend not long ago."

"That's *right*!" I said. I could hardly believe that he remembered and recognized me.

"No need to sound so amazed," he kind of chuckled. "I broke my hip, not my head."

"I'm sorry to hear that," I said. Then I realized how that sounded, like I was sorry he hadn't broken his head. I stammered something out, trying to explain, but he was laughing.

"I guess you're not in a lot of pain or anything," I observed.

"Not now," he said, still grinning. "I was yesterday, all right. It hurt something fierce. Once the surgeon had righted things, though, it was okay. 'Course, they have me on some painkillers, too."

"Well, I'm glad it wasn't anything more serious than a broken bone," I said. "I happened to be walking by your place yesterday when the ambulance came. That's how I knew you were here."

"It was real kind of you to come," he said, his face growing serious. "Time seems to drag along awful slow when you're in the hospital."

"Will your daughter come to see you very often?" I asked.

"Well, she will when she can. She has her job, though, and her kids. Makes it hard for her."

"And what about your cat, Ernie?" I asked. "Is someone taking care of him?"

"Not yet." Worry crept into his eyes. "I was trying to get in touch with Eldred, an old friend of mine, to ask him to look in on the little guy, but I haven't been able to reach him yet."

"I'd be glad to help out, if there's anything I can do," I said.

"Thing about Ernie," Mr. Stanley sighed, "is that he's not used to being alone. I might have mentioned before that he's a bit on the nervous side. I'm sure I can find someone to put food out for him, but what he really needs is to be around people."

"What if I took him to my place until you get

home?" I asked. It occurred to me that it might have been a good idea to check with my folks about that first, but the way Mr. Stanley's face lit up at my words, I decided to worry about that later.

"That'd be ideal!" he said. "He liked you, you know, when you met him at the apartment a little while back. I could tell."

"I liked him, too." I smiled, thinking it seemed a bit preposterous that Mr. Stanley thought he could actually tell whether or not his cat had liked me, but I wasn't about to tell him that.

"Well, that's just grand," he proclaimed. "Takes a load off my mind, I can tell you."

Then he got me to look in the little locker beside his bed. I rummaged through his stuff, which smelled faintly of some kind of aftershave, located his keys in his pants pocket, and stuck them in my own pocket. It was kind of weird to think he was just handing me the keys to his place without knowing anything about me, really.

"He has tins of food in the cupboard under the kitchen sink. Should be a dozen or so there, lots to keep him going until I'm back up and about. There's dry food, too. I leave some out for him most of the time, and he'll eat it, but he prefers the tins."

"Do you have a pet carrier for him?" I thought to ask.

"Yep. In the hall closet, just inside the door. I put him in it when he goes to the V.E.T." He paused and

17

laughed. "I guess I don't need to spell that now, since he's not here. He knows the word, though. I've gotten in the habit of spelling it out so he won't suspect anything when he has to take a trip there."

Right. I suppose when you get on in years, you can start getting a bit shaky in the reality department. I smiled and nodded as though it was normal to think a cat could figure out what you were talking about. No sense hurting the old guy's feelings.

I stayed for a bit longer, but it was clear to me that Mr. Stanley was actually getting anxious for me to leave. I think it was because he was eager to have Ernie taken care of. I gave him a pat on the hand as I was going and told him not to worry about the cat, that I'd take good care of it.

It's funny how our chance encounter earlier in the summer had brought this unexpected cat-sitting job about. You just never know what kind of turns events will take and what they'll end up meaning in your life.

I was thinking about this as I made my way back to the apartment building. I was also thinking that it wouldn't hurt if Mom happened to be in a really good mood when I showed up with a cat.

We haven't had a pet since our dog, Brownie, got hit by a car and died two years ago. I brought the subject up a couple of times, but Mom just said we'd talk about it another time — only we never did. She's not much of a cat person, either. Keeping Ernie at our place isn't going to be an easy sell.

The only thing that might save me is that Mom is kind-natured and won't want to think of it suffering. I'll need to try, without *actually* lying, to make it sound like there were no other options.

When I reached Mr. Stanley's apartment and let myself in, Ernie came along right away, though his movements were cautious and wary. By the way he approached me I could see he was nervous but determined. I guess the little guy had been lonely. It was a relief to see that there was still a bit of dry food in his bowl, though it was pretty low. It looked like I'd gotten there just in time.

I patted him and talked soothingly to reassure him that I wasn't going to harm him. Then I went to fetch the carrier, so I could get him to my house before my mom got home.

I had this vision in my head of getting there and having her standing at the doorway with her arms crossed, shaking her head side to side and telling me there was *no way* that cat was coming inside. I figured that if he was already in, my chances of persuading her to let us babysit him for a while were a lot better.

I found the carrier in the closet, just where Mr. Stanley had said it would be. Getting Ernie into it was another story altogether, let me tell you. The second he saw it, he let out some weird cat screech and took off, hiding behind a big armchair in the living room. I managed to shoo him out of there, but then he took off down the hall and parked himself under the bed, right in the middle where I couldn't reach him.

Reluctantly, I went and got the broom from the kitchen and kind of half swept and half nudged him with it until he got fed up and dashed out of the bedroom. I followed him, remembering to shut the door behind me so he couldn't go back in there.

I won't add to my embarrassment by describing how Ernie tricked me repeatedly and avoided capture over the next forty minutes. Suffice it to say that I *finally* got him into the carrier, tossed some of his things into a bag, and headed home.

After that experience, I figured handling Mom's objections would be a piece of cake.

CHAPTER THREE

"*W*hat on earth is that noise?"

Mom's question wasn't the best possible start to a discussion about my having brought Ernie home. I'd kind of imagined I'd introduce the whole subject over dinner. You know, like I'd start by bringing up poor old Mr. Stanley and then finish up with his cat's plight. I figured it might even prompt Mom to come right out and offer for us to cat-sit the little guy.

So, it was unfortunate that Ernie was setting up a bit of a howl. I guess that was my own fault. The plan had been to leave him in the carrier, in my room, until after I'd had a chance to clear the whole thing with my folks.

Well, it seems that Ernie wasn't all that fond of being left by himself in the miniature prison — not if the unearthly sounds emanating from my bedroom were any indication.

The first one wasn't too loud, but once he got warmed up, look out. It was enough to make your hair stand on end.

"Uh, actually, I wanted to talk to you about that," I stammered.

Mom was giving me one of her penetrating looks, the kind that sees past anything other than the truth, the whole truth, and nothing but the truth. One of her eyebrows lifted. She stood there with her hands on her hips. The look on her face wasn't exactly the kind that invites long, open conversations.

"It's a cat," I said. "I know I shouldn't have brought it here without asking first, but I can explain."

"Mmhmm. Well, I'm waiting."

I did my best to fill her in on what had happened in a way that would play on her sympathies. This was not easy with Ernie's yowls and wails reverberating through the place, making it sound like a haunted house.

"So," I wrapped up, "I just didn't know what else to do. I couldn't leave him there to *starve* to death, could I?"

I turned imploring eyes to Dad, who'd remained silent through the whole story. He gave a bit of a shrug and looked at the floor.

"I don't suppose he'll starve to death if you go over and feed him once a day," Mom pointed out. "And that's exactly what you're going to do."

"But..."

"No buts about it. We're *not* having a cat here."

"Do I have to take him back today?" I asked. Tears were forming, but they were more from anger than anything else. "Couldn't he just have one night here?"

"Making that racket?" Mom didn't exactly look impressed at the idea.

"He's only doing that because he's in a carrier," I said. "If I let him out..."

"If you let him out, he'll shed all over the house. That's the worst thing about cats. Hair everywhere. And they're so sneaky."

I thought of Ernie's cunning escapes when I was trying to get him into the carrier at Mr. Stanley's apartment and couldn't argue with her.

"Well, go get the carrier," Dad spoke at last, "and I'll give you a drive."

I went to my room with a heavy heart. My head was racing, desperately trying to come up with a new, more convincing argument, but I couldn't think of a thing. I trudged slowly back to the living room and sat the carrier on the floor.

"All black," Dad observed. "Cute little fellow anyway."

Mom sniffed the air and very pointedly did *not* look in Ernie's direction.

I sniffed too, wondering if Mom's heart would soften if I burst out crying. She's not that easily fooled, though, and chances were good that would only backfire.

"Now, Shelby," Dad said. "Don't feel bad. You'll get to see the cat, uh, what's its name?"

"Ernie."

"Ernie, huh? Interesting name. Anyway, you'll get to see Ernie every day when you go to feed him. You can always spend a bit of time with him then."

"But he'll be all alone the rest of the time," I lamented.

"Ah, cats don't mind that. They sleep most of the time anyway. No, he'll be the very best. Well, as long as nothing…"

I felt alarm rise in me as his voice trailed off. I demanded to know what he'd been about to say.

"Oh, it's just silly," Dad said. "Nothing really to worry about at all."

"Of course there isn't," my mother added sternly. She still hadn't glanced at Ernie. Not once.

"Well, unless there was, you know, a fire or something. But, as I said, that's not likely at all. Really, what are the odds?"

"A fire!" I gasped. "What if there *was* one! What if Ernie couldn't get out?"

"Oh, for goodness' sake," Mom said, giving her head a shake. For the first time, she took a quick peek at the cat.

"It *could* happen," I cried. "How would I ever tell Mr. Stanley? He *trusted* me to take care of Ernie."

"This Mr. Stanley," Mom frowned, as if the poor old guy had deliberately fallen and hurt himself just to cause her this trouble, "how long is he supposed to be in the hospital?"

"I don't know, not for sure," I admitted. "Probably a few weeks or so."

"And then he'll be back home and able to take care of his cat by himself?"

"Yes."

Mom sighed. She looked at Ernie again, a bit longer. She frowned some more. I was barely breathing.

"I suppose," she said at last, "that if it's only going to be a few weeks, we could put up with the inconvenience."

I opened my mouth, all overjoyed and everything, to tell her thanks. Before I could get so much as a syllable out, she held her hand up and went on.

"However," she said, "this is *entirely* your responsibility, Shelby. Feeding, brushing, cleaning the litter box, extra vacuuming to keep the house from being overrun with floating black hair. All of it. You do it, and I mean *without* being told, or the cat goes."

"I will," I promised. Even though she was trying to sound kind of mean, I threw my arms around her.

Out of the corner of my eye I saw my dad kind of nod and smile the way you do when you have a secret. I suddenly realized that he'd set the whole thing up. I also knew that if I ever brought it up to him, he'd act like he didn't know what I was talking about. My folks have this rule about always backing each other up when it comes to making parenting decisions. It's a real pain sometimes.

But that didn't matter at the moment. Ernie was staying, even if it was only for a few weeks. I could hardly wait to let him out of the carrier.

On this particular subject, I wasn't the only eager one. The second I began to free him, Ernie flew from the dreadful trap. Leaving captivity behind, he formed a black streak that disappeared from the room before I even had the carrier's door fully open.

"He's probably shy," I said, forcing a smile. Mom seemed far from pleased.

"You'd better find him," she said sternly. "I don't want him doing goodness knows what goodness knows where."

I thought of the mad chase he'd taken me on in the apartment earlier in the day, and that was in a place that had only a few small rooms. As I headed down the hallway calling his name, I began to wonder if he was worth all the bother he'd been already.

I found him over an hour later, hidden behind the ironing board in the laundry room. He was crouched there, looking a bit wild and scared. His blue eyes blinked in what seemed like confusion.

I reached a hand out to pat him and was rewarded with a swat, claws out, that made a tiny red path across a couple of my fingers. Nice.

Determined, I reached out again, but by the time my hand got there this time, he'd burst out of his hiding spot. I had no doubt that escape was uppermost in his furry little head, but I'd outsmarted him (for the first time) and closed the door when I'd entered the room, just in case.

Even so, it was a while before I succeeded in picking him up and carrying him to the spare room, which Mom had readied for his stay. Dishes with food and water were lined up along the wall, and a bed had been fashioned on the floor with a couple of old blankets.

I plunked the troublemaker down on the floor and closed the door before he could get away again.

It looked like it was going to be a long two weeks.

Chapter Four

It seems there were a few things Mr. Stanley hadn't thought to mention about Ernie, one of them being he's not the best behaved cat ever, and the other that he's an enormous baby if he's left alone at night. Goodness only knows if any of the other tenants in Mr. Stanley's apartment building got any sleep the night before, when Ernie was there by himself. Maybe he behaved better in his own place where he was used to everything, I don't know.

I do know that he was not what you'd call a model guest at our place. Not by a long shot. He started up not long after Mom had nicely tucked him away with food and water, a fresh litter box, and a cut-down cardboard box lined with old blankets. All the comforts of home, which you'd think would be as much as most cats would expect.

Not Ernie. Maybe he fancies himself kind of high class or something, on account of his sleek and shiny fur, so black that it's almost blue in the light, and his eyes complementing his coat with an almost electric shade of blue if you happen to look at him from certain angles. Whatever his reasons, he sure made it clear he expected better treatment than he was getting, locked up like some kind of prisoner.

The first sign of trouble started with a kind of scraping noise, which I quickly recognized as Ernie clawing at the door. The spare room is close to mine, so I hurried down the hall, opened the door a crack and hissed at him to stop it.

It seemed like he meant to obey, because right away he plunked his behind down on the carpet and started purring really loud. It threw me off guard for a few seconds, considering his performance earlier in the day. I decided he'd realized I was on his side and had made up his mind to treat me better.

"What a *good* cat," I complimented him, reaching a hand in and giving him a quick pat. He rubbed his face up against my fingers and purred louder.

"That's right, you're *such* a good kitty," I repeated. "Well, I guess I'll see you in the morning then." I told him goodnight, stepped back, and shut the door. I almost made it to my room before the scratching started again.

"That cat had better not be clawing at the wood-work," Mom called out from down the hall.

I was back at Ernie's door by then, having another heart-to-heart with him about appropriate behaviour when you're in someone else's home. Judging by the tilt of his head, you'd think he was listening attentively, but you'd be wrong.

By the time Ernie had listened to four lectures and I'd made as many trips back and forth from my room to his, I'd realized the current arrangement wasn't going to work.

"You're not such a good cat after all, are you?" I whispered as I carried him to my room. Then I had to go back and get everything else Mom had fixed up for him. By the time I got it all set up in my room, he was nicely curled up in the middle of my bed.

"*This* is your bed," I explained, plopping him onto the blankets Mom had stuffed into the cardboard box. He purred his thanks and then leapt back onto mine the second my back was turned. I put him back in the box. He jumped back onto my bed and settled down with a huge yawn.

I could see that Ernie hadn't had much in the way of discipline growing up. Probably none, in fact. If tonight was any example, I was willing to bet that Mr. Stanley had spoiled him at every turn.

"Tomorrow," I warned him as he was drifting off to sleep, "you are going to have to learn some of the rules."

I'd intended to sleep in a bit the next morning, seeing as everyone was away and there wasn't much to do. Ernie had other ideas, though. He woke me bright and early with a combination of loud purring and a noisy face wash. You wouldn't think it could be all that loud, a cat licking its paws and rubbing its face, but Ernie managed to do it at maximum volume, slurping and rasping and just generally making disgusting noises.

"Quiet down," I mumbled, stuffing my head under the pillow.

The next thing I knew something was bumping up against me. I peeked out and saw Ernie, the top of his head rammed against my leg, like he'd been giving me a head butt and got stuck.

"You're weird," I informed him. He purred even louder, like I'd just paid him a lovely compliment.

By then, of course, I was wide awake. I decided to get organized and go see Mr. Stanley early, just to put his mind at ease that Ernie was settled in okay.

First, though, his things had to be put wherever they were going to be while he was with us. I sat his dishes in a corner in the kitchen and put the litter box downstairs in the laundry room. I left the bed Mom had made up for him in my room, not that it was likely he'd suddenly start co-operating and use it. Then I showed him where everything was a few times, but he didn't seem to be paying much attention.

"Don't worry about that," Mom told me a bit later. "He's a cat. He'll explore and have the lay of the place in no time. We'll just have to make sure the laundry room door stays open. Otherwise, my big house plants won't be safe."

I headed off to the hospital then, deliberately taking the street that goes past Broderick's Gas Bar where Greg works. It made me miss him even more than I already was, which was a lot.

He and his dad don't really have a firm schedule for how long they're going to stay away, so I can't even count the days left on their vacation.

Betts's boyfriend, Derek, is filling in for Greg while he's away, but it couldn't have been his shift because it was Old Man Broderick who was there when I went by. His thin arm came up in a kind of half-wave as I walked past, and his face broke out into a wide smile. He's a nice old guy and Greg likes working for him.

That reminded me that I should probably start job hunting again pretty soon, but then school will be starting in just a few weeks and I'm not sure I want to have a job during the school year. I'm going into Grade 11 and I know my marks this year are going to count toward university. I'm not sure where I want to go, since I haven't really decided what I want to do — not for sure, anyway. When I do make up my mind, though, I don't want bad grades to keep me from being accepted into the university I pick.

By the time I'd reached the hospital I'd pretty well made up my mind to stick with casual jobs like babysitting for now, even though that's not my favourite way to make money.

Mr. Stanley brightened right up as soon as I entered his room. "How's Ernie?" he asked, leaning forward eagerly.

I told him Ernie was fine and filled him in on the adventures I'd had in getting him to my place and then settling him down for the night.

"He's a bit of a rascal all right," Mr. Stanley said with a big grin. You'd think a person would be just a tiny bit embarrassed to learn of their cat's misbehaviour, but he was beaming with pride.

"Uh, what do you usually do to get him to, you know, behave?" I asked.

He looked puzzled for a few seconds and I was thinking of how I could rephrase the question when he answered.

"If by 'behave' you mean how do I get him to obey," he said, "the answer is, I don't. I'm afraid I may have indulged the little fellow."

While it didn't exactly surprise me to hear him admit that Ernie had been spoiled, I must admit I was a little dismayed. If Ernie had never learned to respond to the word *no* it would be impossible to stop him if he decided, for example, to sharpen his claws on the legs of our oak dining table. I didn't picture Mom taking that very well.

"It's not as if you can train a cat," Mr. Stanley was saying. "Or didn't you know that?"

"I've never had a cat," I said, "but I didn't think they were dumb."

"They're *not* dumb," he said, bristling a little. "In fact, they're too smart to take orders."

I was thinking that Ernie might smart himself right out of a place to stay if he got too much out of line, but I didn't say that to Mr. Stanley. Instead, I changed the subject and hoped for the best.

By the time I'd been there for almost an hour I could see that Mr. Stanley was getting tired, even though he seemed to be enjoying our visit. I promised to stop by again soon and headed home.

I was walking back toward my house when a familiar car drove by. I recognized it right away, which made my mouth fall open and a strange feeling start up in the pit of my stomach.

It was the Thompsons' car, no doubt about it. Even if I hadn't been sure, the fact that Mrs. Thompson was driving it would have confirmed it for me. Only, Betts and her family were supposed to be on holidays for another two weeks!

My head was reeling with questions by the time I got home. There was something very odd going on, and I was going to find out what it was. I made up my mind to go over there right that minute and find out why they were back so far ahead of schedule, and more importantly, why Betts hadn't called to tell me she was home.

Chapter Five

"Shelby!"

It was Mrs. Thompson who answered the door when I got to Betts's place, so I guess she was on her way home when she drove past me. The car was nowhere in sight, though, so I guessed she'd parked in the garage, even though it was summer. Her surprised expression told me she hadn't been expecting to see me.

"Hi, Mrs. Thompson," I said. "Is Betts home?"

"Oh, uh, Betts is, uh, well, I, uh…"

"For goodness' sake, Mom, she knows I'm here," Betts said, appearing in the doorway. "Anyway, I told you, we can trust Shelby."

Mrs. Thompson sighed and stepped back enough to let me in. She didn't look so hot, I noticed. Her face was pale and there were dark circles under her eyes.

"I'm telling her everything," Betts said as she took my arm and pulled me toward the kitchen. Her voice was tired, like she'd had this argument a few times and didn't have the energy to do it again.

"Oh, go ahead," Mrs. Thompson said, sounding just as weary. "It won't be long before all of Little River hears about it, anyway."

My head was spinning by the time we plunked down at the table. Betts opened her mouth to speak a couple of times but couldn't seem to get started. Then, before she got a single word out, she started to cry.

"My mom," she finally sobbed, "is going to jail."

"*What?*" It was probably the last thing I might have guessed she was going to say. "Betts, that's the craziest thing I ever heard. What on earth happened?"

"They think she stole something from work." With a little more control, Betts went on to explain that someone had apparently broken into the secure room at the software development office of NUTEC, where Mrs. Thompson was the manager.

"What was taken?" I asked.

"Some new software line for small businesses. I don't know much about it, but Mom says they've been working on it for quite a while and it was expected to bring in a lot of money. Like, millions. Only now it's been stolen."

"But why do they think your mom had anything to do with it? That's insane!"

VALERIE SHERRARD

"*We* know that, but the police sure don't. I guess it's because everything kind of points toward her."

"What do you mean?"

Betts went through the whole thing from start to finish then. The theft had taken place at night on July 19. Someone had gotten into the locked room — to which Mrs. Thompson had the only key — and had taken the master disks.

The room's second-floor window had been broken, apparently to make it look as though the thief had gotten in that way, but the glass shards were all outside on the ground, proving it had been smashed from the inside.

To make matters even worse, the disks had been taken from a safe to which only Mrs. Thompson knew the combination.

I had to admit that it looked bad, all right.

"So, what's been going on *here*? You guys didn't go on holidays at all?"

"Nah, we've just been sitting around the house like prisoners. Mom only went out today because she had to see her lawyer. I don't think that went well, either, because she was pretty upset when she got home."

"I don't understand the point of this business of keeping out of sight."

"Me neither. Mom just went kind of weird when this whole thing started, and she said the best thing we could do was lie low and hope the police found the real

38

thief. We're supposed to be on vacation right now, so she thinks that's what everyone will assume."

"Why didn't you go? I mean, you might as well be away somewhere that you don't have to think about this day and night."

"Yeah, only the police kind of told Mom not to leave town."

"That's horrible."

"I didn't do it."

Betts and I both swung around to see Mrs. Thompson standing in the doorway to the kitchen. Her voice had been small and timid, but she repeated the words in a louder, stronger tone.

"I didn't do it."

"Well, *we* know that, Mom." Betts offered a smile but it came out kind of lopsided.

"Of course we do," I chimed in.

"I don't suppose it will matter who believes me if I'm convicted anyway."

"You won't be, Mom," Betts said quickly. "You're innocent!"

"So was David Milgaard," she said grimly.

"Who?" Betts and I asked in unison.

"David Milgaard. He was wrongfully convicted of raping and killing a student nurse named Gail Miller back in 1969."

"What happened to him?"

"He spent nearly twenty-three years in prison for a crime he didn't commit. His mother fought to get him a new trial, and he was eventually exonerated."

"Ex-what-ed?" Betts asked.

"Exonerated. It means cleared."

"Twenty-three *years* in prison?" I couldn't quite believe it.

"That's right. So, innocence doesn't always guarantee justice. Mistakes can be made, especially in a situation like this, where the evidence seems so overwhelming."

I realized, with a start, that she was frightened. That was something new, to see an adult scared that way.

"And now Zuloft, *my own lawyer*, tells me if I'm charged, and he believes I will be, we can plead this down and I'll probably just get probation. Nice to know the person who'd be defending me doesn't even believe in me, though of course he insists he does, and that he's just obligated to explain my options."

"Fire him and get someone else," Betts said.

"I've already given him a hefty deposit," she said heavily. "If I fired him now, I'd probably lose most of it."

"Will your lawyer be looking for evidence to help clear you?" I asked.

"Supposedly, though I get the feeling that he's more committed to his fee than he is to me."

"You should get Shelby to investigate," Betts said suddenly, jumping up in excitement at the idea. "She's really good at figuring things out."

"Betts..." I began.

"Now, Betts, I don't..." her mom also began.

Betts cut both of us off.

"I know what you're both going to say, but think about it. It's perfect! You can send her in as a summer student and she can find out what really happened."

"A summer student?" I parroted. I must admit the idea was starting to sound kind of intriguing. It hadn't taken that long to catch my interest, either.

"Even if I did that," Mrs. Thompson said, "how would that help to catch the real thief?"

"I guess Betts is assuming it's an inside job," I jumped in. "That pretty much makes sense, considering how much the person had to know about the place."

"That would mean one of my employees is responsible," Mrs. Thompson said, shaking her head. "I just don't believe it."

"Then it would be good to clear them completely," I said. The more it was discussed, the more I wanted to get into that office and start nosing around. "Besides, even if it was totally an outsider, that person might have left clues, or maybe they got information somehow from someone who works at NUTEC."

"What kind of information?"

"Oh, like casual questions about the place's security measures or things like that. You can ask a lot of things without arousing the least bit of suspicion, if you do it in an innocent way."

Mrs. Thompson was nodding then, and I could tell she was beginning to really consider Betts's suggestion. I kind of held my breath, waiting for her decision.

"Well, I don't suppose it can hurt anything," she said at last. "I don't have much else to lose."

Not exactly the greatest vote of confidence I've ever gotten, but I didn't care. I was in, and I had a new mystery to look into.

Betts squealed and danced around like the whole thing was already solved and settled. She was so happy that it made me uncomfortable. After all, it wasn't as though she actually had anything to be relieved over. I hadn't done anything, and there was no guarantee that I'd be able to.

I almost regretted getting caught up in the whole idea. I'd just taken on more responsibility than I'd realized, and now my best friend was counting on me to make everything okay.

What if I failed?

CHAPTER SIX

Mrs. Thompson arranged for me to start at NUTEC the very next day. She still had two more weeks off for her regular vacation time, although she didn't even know if she'd be able to go back when that time was up. She'd talked to the owners but they hadn't said much one way or the other.

"I got the impression they were hoping the police would have something solid by the end of my holidays," she told me, "so that if I did it, they could let me go without looking as though they were jumping the gun.

"Since I may not be going back at all, I'd better get you in there right away, while I still have some authority."

"You won't tell anyone why I'm coming, though, right?" I asked.

"Oh, I trust the people I work with," Mrs. Thompson said. It sounded as though she was trying to persuade herself as much as me. "I don't believe for a minute that this is an inside job. But I won't let them know what you're doing there. As far as anyone is concerned, you'll just be a student working through a summer employment project."

"Most likely you're right about the thief being someone from outside the company," I said slowly, "but I quite honestly can't take a single chance. You've just told me that the theft is going to cost your company millions of dollars. For that kind of money, the guilty person could be willing to do something desperate if he or she felt threatened.

"The thing is," I continued, "if no one knows why I'm there, they can't accidentally let something slip and give me away to anyone else — employee *or* outsider. I want to help, I really do, but I don't want to take any risks I can avoid."

Not long ago I'd put myself in a pretty dangerous predicament. The scare hadn't quite worn off yet, and I was determined not to get in that kind of spot again if I could help it.

Mrs. Thompson seemed to understand. At least she promised that no one would hear about it from her.

Betts was another worry, because she's a huge fan of gossip — the juicier the better. She did give me her word, though, and I think she realized how important secrecy was in this situation. Besides, if she told anyone about what I was doing, she'd have to explain why, and that would be embarrassing for her own mother.

"It would be helpful if you'd tell me a little bit about each person who works there," I said then, "so I don't have to waste time figuring out who's who and who does what. If I know what everyone is *supposed* to do, it might help me pick up on it if any of them do something unusual."

Mrs. Thompson repeated her earlier opinion that none of her staff were involved, but she told me a little bit about each employee anyway. I wrote down their names, underlined them, and scribbled bits of information as she spoke.

Darla Rhule. Project Manager and also in charge during Mrs. Thompson's absence. Employed for the past 22 years, very good at her job. Married with three grown children. No obvious financial problems — both she and her husband have good incomes.

"When you meet Darla you'll be struck by how organized and energetic she is. She just never seems to stop, which keeps some of the younger employees on their toes."

James Rankin. Accounting and Bookkeeping. He and his wife are childless and both are employed so money problems are unlikely.

"You might expect someone in that field to be stern or dull." Mrs. Thompson smiled for the first time since we'd begun talking. "James is nothing like that, though. He's laid-back and good-natured. He does his work efficiently, though without the passion you'll see in the staff who have more creative jobs."

Angi Alexander. Graphic Artist. Mid-thirties, made a career change after four years as the NUTEC secretary. Went back to school to learn her new trade and was rehired on graduation, first as the assistant. Last year when the main designer left for another job, Angi took over. Talented, upbeat, and generally pleasant. Appears to live on a fairly tight budget but doesn't complain or seem focused on money.

"You tell Angi you'd like to see a certain design and she works it up for you, but sometimes you look at it and you just know it's not right, even though it's what you asked for. Some artists might not take that well, but Angi just shrugs and starts something else. She really seems to love her new job."

Janine LeBlanc. Secretary. Chronically behind schedule, though more from mismanagement of her time than overwork.

I'd be sent in to work as Janine's assistant for the remainder of the summer holidays, which would give me the opportunity to have regular contact with all the staff, as well as fairly free access to the common areas.

"Janine is sweet enough, but she's a bit of a news-bag," Mrs. Thompson sighed. "Try to ignore the steady stream of gossip and you'll be better off. If she thinks she has an interested ear it only gets worse."

Contrary to this advice, I made a mental note to look as interested as I could. The more I heard about what went on among the employees at NUTEC, the better my chances were of stumbling on to something important.

Debbie and Stuart Yaeger. Software Developers. Debbie is competent but with an exaggerated opinion of her own abilities while Stuart is the more talented of the two but very quiet and modest. With both of them taking home excellent wages from NUTEC, it seems unlikely that they have any money worries.

"The odd couple," Mrs. Thompson said. "You'd never in a million years expect them to be married to each other, but they've been together since they were in university and they seem to get along just fine. They share the largest office, which, surprisingly enough, works out all right."

Joey Sands. Software Developer. The youngest staff member. A computer genius but not terribly reliable. He designed the stolen program. Financially, he seems less stable than the others. He receives a good salary and generous bonuses from NUTEC but is often broke and borrows small amounts of money between paydays.

"Sometimes he misses work without calling in. He's also a bit moody, and while he's usually sweet and charming, he can be quite cranky. That's probably just because of his age. No doubt he has girlfriend problems at times. I'm sure he's harmless enough."

<u>*Carol Coppice*</u>. *Office Assistant. This is the newest staff member, a forty-something-year-old woman hired through a government make-work program for people who have been unemployed for a long time. She does simple tasks like making photocopies, shredding old documents, and running errands.*

"I'm afraid she's not very likable," Mrs. Thompson said, "though we all make an effort to overlook some of her habits because, as you'll easily see, she's somewhat, uh, limited. Having an office job seems to have made her feel terribly significant and she goes about with a blustery, self-important attitude. She *always* has something to say, but sadly not much of it is worth hearing, which can be very annoying.

"I don't know if this is worth mentioning or not, but we did have a computer programming student from the college in Viander doing a field placement up to a few weeks before the robbery. His name is Gary Todd, but I understand he had a job to go to in Saint John right after his placement was finished, so he wasn't even in the area at the time the theft occurred."

I added his name to the list, just in case.

Later on, back home and in my room, I looked over the list of employees again, trying to conjure up mental images of each one. It was silly, but I felt kind of disappointed that none of the names jumped out at me. Mrs. Thompson's descriptions hadn't made anyone stand out as a potential criminal.

The only one who seemed a possibility at all was Joey Sands, partly because he'd designed the program and might view it as belonging to him, and partly because he was the only one who had a noticeable shortage of funds from time to time. It wasn't much to go on, though, and certainly not enough for me to consider him a definite suspect without some actual evidence.

After memorizing as much information from the list as my brain would absorb just then, I folded the paper and slid it into my desk drawer.

As I got ready for bed, I couldn't help thinking of Betts and how trusting and confident she was that I'd be able to figure this whole mess out. Clicking off my light and crawling under the sheet, I wondered what I'd gotten myself into.

CHAPTER SEVEN

I might as well admit that I was nervous when I walked into the NUTEC offices the next morning. My main goal at that moment was to look calm and nonchalant, but if you've ever tried that you know it's not as easy as it sounds. I'm pretty sure the effort made the expression on my face appear mildly insane rather than casual.

"You must be Shelby," the receptionist said as I approached her desk, trying to walk in a carefree manner and nearly tripping over my own feet in the process.

"Yes." I searched my brain for something smooth and breezy to add, but came up blank.

"So, you're gonna help out around here for the rest of the summer, huh?"

"Yes," I said with a smile, knowing it was coming out lopsided, "I am."

"Cool. I can sure use some help. There's no way one person can handle the phones, do the filing, *and* type letters, but they expect me to. I think they're so used to computers that they think humans can work at the same speed." She arched an eyebrow as if to ask what I thought of that but went on before I had time to formulate a comment.

"I hope you know shorthand, though I don't suppose you do. What are you, sixteen, seventeen? You don't take that kinda stuff in high school, do you? I know I didn't. Anyway, no biggie, I can take dictation and give you other things to do. It's not like there isn't enough work to go around." She leaned back in her chair and ran ring-laden fingers through her long blonde-streaked pale brown hair.

"We'd better get you a chair," she yawned, holding her hands out and looking them over critically, like you do when you've just polished your nails. "You can't stand around all day. By the way, I'm Janine."

I'd gathered that in the first moment there, but I nodded and said, "Hi, Janine," as though I were hearing it for the first time.

"Hello?"

I turned to see that the greeting had come from a slender woman with greying hair who looked to be at least a few years older than my mother. She was dressed in a blue suit and short heels that clicked on the floor as she walked toward me. She held her hand out and I took it awkwardly, feeling a bit silly as she pumped it firmly in a strong handshake.

"Darla Rhule," she said with a smile that flashed for a second and was gone. "I assume you're Shelby. We're glad to have you here for the rest of the summer. If you have any questions or problems feel free to come and see me. Janine will fill you in on what you're expected to do."

Without waiting for me to respond to anything she'd said, Darla hurried down the hall, tap-tap-tapping all the way to an office on the left. She closed the door as soon as she'd crossed the threshold.

Voices behind me caught my attention as a man and woman came along. At first I thought it must be the Yaegers, but when they introduced themselves I discovered they were James Rankin and Angi Alexander. Both greeted me in a friendly way but neither stopped to chat before heading to their offices.

"No one's talking much these days," Janine sighed, looking sad. "Everyone's all nerved up because of the robbery. Well, you wouldn't know anything about that, though, would you? 'Course not. You just started here."

She leaned forward, fluffing her hair for a second time. "I don't suppose there's any reason I can't tell you about it. There was a break-in a couple of weeks ago. Or it was made to *look* like a break-in anyway. Me, I think it was an inside job."

The last sentence was delivered in a secretive tone, which almost made me laugh. From what Mrs. Thompson had told me, everyone was aware of the fact that the window had been broken from the inside. It was one of the strongest pieces of evidence against her, and I figured it would be the one that was the most difficult to explain away. After all, if she was the only person with access to the room and safe, both of which had been opened with apparent ease, it was going to be hard to prove her innocence.

That might have been the first time it occurred to me that maybe she was guilty. As soon as the thought entered my mind, I felt horrible, like I'd betrayed my best friend by suspecting her mother.

What if she *was* guilty, though? If I uncovered evidence that proved it absolutely, what was I going to do? I pushed the uncomfortable thought out of my head and tried to pay attention to Janine again.

"It's enough to give you the creeps, all right," she was saying. "Imagine if there's a criminal right in our midst."

"Do the police have any suspects?" I asked.

"Well, sort of, but I think they're on the wrong track. It's not like they've arrested anyone or laid charges or anything. See, they can only go by what they find when they investigate," she said with a wise nod, "but they don't know the person, so they only have part of the story, if you know what I mean."

"No one ever knows what you mean, Janine." This remark came from a guy who didn't look to be much older than me, though he had to be in his mid-twenties. My assumption that this must be Joey Sands was confirmed almost immediately.

"Joey, this is Shelby." Janine jerked her head in my direction. "She's going to be my assistant for the summer."

"Nice to meet you." Joey smiled and shook my hand. "I can't imagine what you'll be doing, though, if you're supposed to be assisting Janine. How do you help someone do nothing?"

Janine swatted at him, but he easily dodged her hand, laughed, wished me luck, and sauntered off toward his office.

All I could think was that neither of them seemed terribly concerned about the recent robbery. It was also interesting that Janine was so sure Mrs. Thompson was innocent.

I wasn't about to jump to any conclusions, but it seemed that these details were worth noting. I had a small memo pad in my pocket so I could jot things down throughout the day, not trusting that I'd remember everything if I waited until I was home.

With Janine right there, a mental note would have to do for the moment, but I was sure I'd have lots of chances to keep up with note-taking. It's been helpful to me a few times in the past.

"So, is that everyone who works here?" I asked innocently, wondering where the others were.

"Nope. Besides the ones you met there's Carol and Debbie and Stuart. They're married. Debbie and Stuart, that is. Carol's not in yet, but I'm pretty sure the other two are in their office. They've been coming in early a lot lately. Must be working on some big project."

Carol didn't show up for another half an hour. Janine had just put a call through to Stuart Yaeger and I was still waiting for instructions for my first task.

"Don't even think about starting with me." Carol glared at Janine before anyone had said so much as a single word to her. "I had trouble with my car, and anyway, I work harder than anyone else in this building so if I'm late once in a while I shouldn't have to defend myself."

"I couldn't care less if you were late every day," Janine retorted. "Don't come in here hassling me."

"I don't answer to you anyway," Carol snapped back. She seemed to pause when she caught sight of me but didn't bother waiting for an introduction before she stomped off down the hall.

"Well, that was Carol." Janine rolled her eyes but didn't say anything more just then.

"Does she have an office?" I wondered aloud.

"Nope. She works mostly in the copy room. Makes copies, shreds things, gets stuff ready to mail, that kind of thing. She's here to free up the computer geeks from tasks like that so they can concentrate on the important stuff."

"Is she always like that?" I asked cautiously.

"Pretty much. She's here on some kind of government program for people who aren't very employable. I don't see that much of her, thank goodness."

"Do you spend much time with the others?" I asked, wondering when I was going to have a chance to see the rest of the place. So far, we'd stayed in the reception area, and aside from a couple of phone calls, which Janine had taken, we hadn't done anything.

Before she could answer me, a red light appeared on Janine's phone. She pressed a button and I heard a female voice tell her she was needed to take dictation.

"You sure you don't know shorthand?" she sighed as she stood up. "Well, you might as well come along anyway. There's not much you can do here."

She pressed a couple of buttons on the phone, grabbed a steno pad from a drawer, and went off toward Darla's office with me in tow.

The older woman sat behind a huge wooden desk, the surface of which was cluttered with files and books and loose sheets of paper. She offered another brief smile and pointed me to a chair where I sat and watched while Janine scribbled strange-looking symbols on her pad.

The letter being dictated seemed boring, but I forced myself to listen while trying to look fascinated with the office. Darla sure didn't believe in making her work area too cozy, so there wasn't much to look at. The place was practically bare except for a fluffy fern and a professionally done photo of her with her husband and children, both perched on top of a bookcase along the wall. The plant looked a bit droopy.

"Would you like your fern watered?" I asked once Janine was finished.

Darla glanced up at me with a smile. "Thanks, but I kind of like to take care of it myself, silly as that is. Nice to see that you're taking a bit of initiative, though."

CHAPTER EIGHT

While Janine typed up the letter back at her desk my thoughts drifted to the conversation I'd had with my parents the night before. It hadn't gone quite as I'd hoped.

They'd been fine with my announcement that I was going to work at NUTEC, but things got a little tense when it became clear to them that I hadn't told them the entire truth. I honestly don't know why I try to hide stuff from them, since it never works. I must have some subconscious desire to embarrass myself.

"How nice," Mom had said in reply to my news. "It will probably be fun for you — working with Betts's mom."

"Well, uh, she won't be there, actually," I stammered, making it abundantly clear that something was up.

"No? Oh, they're on holidays, aren't they," Mom deduced on her own. "But then, how did she arrange for the job for you if she's out of town?"

"They didn't go away this summer," I said. Of course that just brought a fresh onslaught of questions. Why hadn't I had any contact with Betts for the past two weeks if her family was right here in Little River? Why hadn't the Thompsons gone away as they do every year?

There were more, but I knew after the first few that there was nothing for it but to tell the whole story and hope they didn't forbid me from getting involved. There'd been plenty of discussion, let me tell you, and it was close, but I managed to convince them that it wasn't a dangerous situation.

A bigger question came at the end of that whole conversation, namely, why hadn't I told them the entire truth in the first place.

"It's hard for us to trust that you're making good decisions when you hide things from us," Dad pointed out.

I insisted that I was just trying to protect Mrs. Thompson's privacy, which *was*, after all, part of it. Dad looked a bit sad and disappointed anyway, and that really bothered me.

"Earth to Shelby." Janine's words penetrated my drifting thoughts, and I drew myself back to the present to find her staring at me curiously. I blushed and cast about in my head for something to say to cover my distractedness.

I was about to blurt out some inane comment when I saw that it wasn't really necessary, since Janine had apparently lost interest almost immediately and gone back to her nails. I was starting to wonder when she was going to get some work done, and more importantly, when she was going to give *me* something to do.

As if she'd read my mind, she nodded toward a pair of stacked baskets on her desk marked *IN* and *OUT*. "You can get the letters in the 'out' file ready for the mail," she said. "Type and print out the labels first. You'll find envelopes in the third drawer of my filing cabinet."

I picked up the stack of correspondence that was waiting to be mailed. "Uh, where will I type the labels?" I asked, since Janine was sitting in front of the only computer in the reception area.

"Oh, yeah," she giggled and rolled her eyes. "I guess you need something to type on."

I waited while she thought this problem through. It was obvious to me even after such a short time that there was no hurrying Janine.

"I know," she said at last. "You can use the spare computer in the conference room. It's probably still locked, since no one has used it yet today. I'll get Darla to open it up for you."

I followed her down the hall, carrying the letters that needed mailing and a handful of envelopes to go with them. Waiting outside Darla's office, I listened as Janine explained why she needed the room opened.

"Don't touch anything else in here," Janine told me once Darla had unlocked the door and switched on the fluorescent ceiling lights.

As I sat down at the computer I wondered what she thought I was going to touch. From the quick glance I'd taken around, there didn't exactly seem to be much to get into.

The desk where I found myself working was in the corner to the right of the only window in the room — a large, single-pane sort that didn't open. On the other side of the window was a water cooler, and past that, a small safe sat in the corner opposite mine.

A row of filing cabinets ran behind me, lengthwise along the wall. They were all locked, though a few books were held upright by thick bookends that appeared to be made of stone. If there was such a thing as a decorating theme in the room, stone seemed to be it.

A big stone eagle, wings spread, sat in a pre-flight perch in the centre of the long table that ran most of the length of the room. The table was otherwise bare.

An even larger stone carving, this one of a wolf, sat on the floor along the other wall, its head raised and its jaws open in a silent howl. This piece looked far smoother than the eagle, which had a rough-hewn look, while the wolf seemed almost shiny. It was darker, too, and looked like it would be cool to the touch.

Disappointed that there was so little to see in the room where the robbery had occurred, I turned my attention back to the task I'd been given. None too soon, either, because Janine stuck her head in the doorway a few moments later to ask if I was almost finished.

"Uh, well, I'm getting there," I hedged.

"Good, because apparently one of those letters — from Stuart to some company called Dymelle Enterprises — was supposed to go out on Friday. He was just asking about it. He says heads will roll if it doesn't get there in time. Hurry, or he'll kill us both."

The threat to my life seemed a bit unfair since I hadn't even been there Friday, but I hastened to find the letter and get it ready to mail.

"Better send it Xpresspost," Janine told me as soon as it was in the envelope. "I see that it's only going to Saint John, so it will just cost a few bucks, and that way Stuart will never know we didn't send it when we were supposed to."

Again, I didn't see how she'd managed to make me a partner for the blame since this was something *she'd* neglected to do the week before, but I said nothing and set out for the post office.

As soon as I was out of sight of the NUTEC building, I pulled the notepad out of my pocket and jotted down the few things I'd learned so far. None of them seemed very important, but you never knew.

Remembering that the student — I searched my memory but could only get his first name, Gary, to come to the surface — had gone to Saint John, I wondered if this important letter had anything to do with him. If so, was there a tie between the student and Stuart Yaeger, and if so, what did it mean?

"Don't jump to any conclusions!" I told myself firmly. Still, I added the address of Dymelle Enterprises to my notes, just in case.

CHAPTER NINE

I was engrossed in thoughts of the robbery when I got back to NUTEC, which is how I managed to walk straight into the stone wolf in the conference room. Luckily, my instincts kicked in faster than my brain seemed to be working, and I grabbed it before it could topple over. It was heavy, but I managed to right it okay. I noticed that the depression in the carpet where the base had left an imprint didn't quite line up with the wolf's current placement, which suggested that someone else had walked into it, knocked it right over, and then hadn't quite gotten it back in the same spot. At least I wasn't the only klutz.

I figured it would have made quite a loud crash, carpet or not, and considered myself very fortunate not to have attracted any unnecessary attention.

Then it occurred to me that maybe the wolf had

been knocked over during the robbery. The safe was in the corner past it, so the robber would have needed to walk past the wolf. Anyone familiar with the place would have known about the wolf, though, and therefore shouldn't have knocked it over. That might shoot down the theory of an inside job.

Or it could simply mean that the culprit had an outside accomplice. And, of course, it could have been knocked over at some other time and have nothing to do with the robbery. There were just so many possibilities; narrowing down ideas was going to be rough.

I finished typing the rest of the labels and getting the letters all ready to mail, and I might as well confess that I had a quick peek at each of them before stuffing them into their envelopes. I wished I'd thought to do that with the "urgent" letter I'd just mailed to Dymelle Enterprises. Too late now.

There was nothing that caught my attention, but then I didn't suppose the thief was likely to send off any correspondence that would give him or her away. At least, not from the office.

The smell of nail polish was in the air and Janine was blowing on her fingertips when I got back to the reception area.

"Thank goodness you're done," she said. "The phone never stopped the whole time you were doing that, and we have to start on this month's billing."

"Will I need to do address labels for the bills?"

"No, those are mostly saved on a file and they print automatically. There might be a few new accounts, but they would just need to be added to the billing program."

"What can I do?" I asked.

She took about fifteen minutes to show me how to input details that had been submitted by (as she insisted on calling them) the computer geeks. I was surprised to discover that, in addition to developing software, NUTEC also managed a large website program. Companies, both big and small, paid them to create and maintain websites, with varying fees for services.

Some of the accounts were the same from month to month, and those companies were billed a flat rate depending on the size of the site. Anyone who'd had updates or changes was billed the flat rate plus specific fees for the work done. The billing program did most of the work; our main task was to type in the correct codes, click "update," and then print.

I kept an eye out for Dymelle Enterprises, but it didn't appear on the billing list. If only I'd been nosier when I was mailing the letter earlier. How was I going to help clear Mrs. Thompson if I didn't take advantage of every opportunity to gather information?

Promising myself I'd be a better snoop from then on, I did my best to eavesdrop on Janine's phone calls while I worked. Most of them she just put through to the workers' offices.

Some calls were clearly personal, but I listened to them anyway, just in case. I didn't learn anything about the robbery, but I did find out that her sister is a back-stabbing lowlife who makes moves on Janine's boyfriends, and that her neighbour deserves to be shot for listening to country and western music at full volume. I also noticed that she casually mentioned Joey a couple of times, which made me think she might be kind of interested in him.

At four minutes before twelve o'clock, Janine pushed a button on the phone and stood up, stretching and yawning like she was just waking up.

"Time for lunch," she said. "We can keep working on those after we eat."

As I followed her along the hall, I wondered whether "we" would turn out to mean "me" again, as had been happening since my arrival. The lunchroom, located right across the hall from the conference room, was the only area I'd seen so far that wasn't a soft ecru colour. It was done in an antique yellow wash with burgundy and teal accents.

"Different decorator?" I asked, looking around at the striking effect.

"Debbie designed this." Janine smiled. "Nice, isn't it? The workers that did it were fast, too. Just a few days and it was done. Good thing, because everything was a mess with the room torn apart."

"Where'd everyone eat then?" I asked.

"At our desks," she said. "I hated that, it was so boring. Plus the microwave was in the Yaegers' office and the fridge was stuck in the conference room. It wasn't exactly convenient if you wanted something hot or cold."

"How long ago was it done?"

"I dunno, three, four weeks, I guess. Wait, it was right around the time of the robbery. I remember because water leaked all over the carpet in the conference room and we didn't know if the fridge was doing it or if it was the water cooler."

"And which was it?"

"The repairman couldn't find anything wrong with either of them, so he said it was probably the fridge. Like, something leaked out from it being moved around or tipped the wrong way or whatever. He must have been right 'cause it never happened again."

"Huh," I said, which might not have made me sound much like a brilliant detective. To be honest, it was only day one and I was already discouraged. Short of someone jumping up and confessing, I didn't see how I was going to figure this one out. Not with leaky fridges and urgent letters as my only clues.

Carol was the next to arrive for lunch. She made a big production of seating herself as far away from us as possible, then opened a brown paper bag and pulled out a sandwich wrapped in waxed paper. It looked like the twin of what Janine was eating, a thin slice of ham on white bread. I felt a bit smug chomping into my thick sandwich of tuna with chopped celery on whole wheat.

Joey and the Yaegers wandered in next, and I noticed that Janine sat up a little straighter and seemed much more animated. Remembering her comments about a boyfriend earlier, I wondered if perhaps they had a secret relationship. There was no sign of anything like that from him, but then he might just be better at hiding things.

Angi sailed in a moment later, breezing by with a burst of friendly chatter directed, it seemed, at everyone in general and no one in particular.

"I just don't know," she said, waving her hand dramatically, "how one person can be so creative. I believe I might be a genius of some sort."

"All that and beauty too," Stuart said dryly. This earned him an elbow in the side from his wife, but then she laughed and patted the seat beside her for Angi to join them.

"I suppose," Angi slid into the seat, "you're all dying to know what brilliant design I've come up with this time."

"Not really." This came from Joey, who was opening a container of yoghurt. "But you're going to force it on us, so we might as well get it over with."

"Those two will kill each other one of these days," Janine hissed into my ear.

"Ha! You'd just love that, wouldn't you?" Angi said with a toss of her head. "Like I'm going to talk about it in front of a thieving scoundrel such as yourself."

I could hardly believe my ears! She'd just out-and-out called Joey a thief, right in front of everybody. I snuck a furtive peek at him to see how he was reacting, but he seemed remarkably undisturbed.

"You, Angi dear, wouldn't know what to do with a unique idea if it smacked you in the forehead," he tossed back, plunging his spoon into the yoghurt. "We couldn't possibly expect you to recognize originality in others."

This remark earned him a grape, which Angi hurled at him from her seat. He caught it easily and popped it into his mouth with a smile.

"Surely we haven't sunk to the puerile level of having food fights." Darla stood in the doorway, arms folded and one eyebrow raised. In spite of her serious tone and stance, there was a slight twitch at the corner of her mouth, and I could tell she was just barely keeping herself from laughing.

"Food fights?" Angi echoed innocently, getting ready to lob another grape even as she spoke. "Of course not."

Another grape flew through the air, but too high, and Joey had to half-stand to catch it. He popped it into his yoghurt dish and stirred.

While Angi and Joey continued the playful combat throughout lunch, I heard Janine let out a barely audible but obviously longing sigh.

CHAPTER TEN

I spent the rest of the day working on the bills while Janine managed to look busy without actually (as far as I could see) accomplishing anything. She kept up a steady stream of chatter between talking on the phone and telling me bits of gossip about the various staff members. Unfortunately, none of it was likely to be helpful in my investigation, unless the fact that Carol wore dreadful colour combinations or that James smoked cigarillos on the sly somehow figured into the solution.

James hadn't joined us in the lunchroom, and I wondered if he'd kept working and eaten at his desk, or maybe gone out somewhere to eat, or what the story was, but I didn't want to ask any more questions than I already had. It was true that Janine seemed only too happy to have something to talk about, but too much curiosity was bound to strike her as odd at some point.

By quitting time I'd learned nothing that seemed the least bit helpful. If anything, the bits of information I'd gathered throughout the day were likely to confuse me. It was pretty discouraging.

It's only the first day, I reminded myself, but that did little to cheer me. Mrs. Thompson was supposed to go back to work in two weeks, and it was vital that her name be cleared before then.

I'd promised Betts and her mom that I'd stop by on my way home each day, but somehow I wasn't all that eager to admit that I hadn't made the slightest progress. It was probably for that reason I popped into the hospital to see Mr. Stanley first.

He was propped up, with the top of his bed raised, and his dinner was there on a tray but it was almost untouched.

"Aren't you hungry?" I asked as I plunked down in the visitor's chair beside the bed.

"I *was*," he grumbled, "but this here food, if you can even call it that, ain't fit to eat. Ruined my appetite."

I looked at the dinner plate, where a thin slice of meat lay in congealed, nearly transparent gravy. Beside it, limp green beans sat in a puddle of water next to a blob of mashed potatoes. I saw that he'd taken a few bites but most of it was undisturbed. I have to admit it didn't exactly look appetizing.

"It looks cold," I said slowly. "Maybe there's some-where I could heat it up for you."

"Nah," he said, "it was warm when it got here. It just doesn't taste like real food."

"Is there anything I could get for you? From the cafeteria, maybe?" I asked.

"Thanks, little one," he said, "but it's probably all the same. I'll have a bite of toast later. Anyway, how's Ernie?"

"He's fine." I smiled to show I meant it. "A bit headstrong, maybe."

"He is at that," Mr. Stanley chuckled. "But he's still a fine fellow underneath it all. I'm awful thankful you're taking care of him."

"The days must be long for you in here," I said after we'd chatted for a few more minutes. "Would you like me to bring something for you to read?"

"Well, now, I think I would," he said, nodding. "If it's not too far out of your way, would you stop at the library and get me *Seventeen* by Booth Tarkington?"

I'd never heard of either the book or the author, so I hauled out my notepad and scribbled them down, told him I'd do my best to have it for him the next day, and left. The thought of his cold, dismal dinner made me stop in the hallway and add "fruit and snacks" underneath his book request.

I stopped to call Mom before continuing on to the Thompsons' house, just to let her know I'd be late for dinner. She asked how my first day had gone, said she'd put a plate in the fridge for me to reheat later, then told me she and Dad were going to the Austers' place to play Canasta.

As I made my way along Hubert Street, I couldn't help thinking that Mom was starting to loosen up a bit. There was a time not too long ago when she'd have asked me a thousand questions about why I was going to be late, where I was going, how long I'd be there, and on and on. It used to drive me crazy, so it was kind of strange how I felt almost, well, sad that she'd let up on the interrogations. It's not like I was feeling sorry for myself or thinking she just didn't care anymore or anything crazy like that. Just that it was a bit strange to be treated less and less like her little girl. Which, of course, I no longer am.

Anyway, I got to the Thompsons' house and went around to the side door, which everyone uses. Betts answered my knock, shoved the door open, and turned away as I stepped inside.

"Something wrong?" I asked.

"Yeah," she said, her voice heavy and helpless. "The police arrested Mom."

"No!"

"About three hours ago. They took her to the station, but Dad went down too because they said she'd be released once the charges were laid. Then I think they

said she'll have to go to court for a plea or trial or however it works. I wasn't listening all that carefully, if you
want the truth. Do you know anything about that stuff?"

"No, not really. Anyway, that's down the road. The
best thing to do is deal with things as they happen and
not worry too much about what's supposed to happen
later. Did your mom call her lawyer to meet her at the
police station?"

"I think she told Dad to do that when they were taking her to the car. Can you imagine!" Betts's voice suddenly quavered and her mouth trembled as tears began.
"My mom! In jail! I just can't believe it. Why can't they
see that there's no way she did something like that?"

By the time she'd managed to get that much out,
she'd broken right down and was sobbing too hard to
say anything further. My heart went out to her, and I
hugged her until she finally stopped.

"It just feels so unreal, you know?" she said softly.
"How can they even think that about her? I mean,
why would my mother do something like that? She is
not a criminal!"

"I wish I knew what to say," I said, feeling as helpless as she'd sounded earlier. "I can't imagine how hard
this must be for all of you."

It was true, too, I couldn't. I tried to visualize my
own mother being arrested and charged with a crime,
but the idea was so ludicrous I couldn't summon any

kind of mental picture of it. Of course, last week I'd have said that nothing like this could possibly happen to Betts's mom, either.

What I *could* understand was why it would be almost easy for the police to believe Mrs. Thompson was guilty. Not only did the evidence point straight at her, but the temptation of that much money created an obvious motive. The only consolation in that thought was knowing that kind of motive would apply to anyone.

Not wanting to leave her alone, I stayed with Betts for the next hour and we talked about the whole thing, but it was like going around and around in circles.

I had intended to leave right away when Mr. and Mrs. Thompson arrived home. Instead, I found that Mrs. Thompson really wanted to see me.

"Shelby, I've told my lawyer about you, that you're working at NUTEC and trying to see what you can find out from inside the office. He thinks I'm quite mad, I'm sure, but I made it clear I'm not budging on this. At least he's not still talking about taking a plea bargain, but he's got who knows how many cases, and every conversation we have, he manages to bring up money one way or another.

"So, I instructed him to copy the file for you. Every document, photo, every last scrap of evidence. He's to have it ready for you tomorrow and I'll send Keith to pick it up. I'll give it to you when you come by after leaving NUTEC."

"There won't be any problem for me to keep working there?" I asked. It seemed possible that now that she'd been charged officially she'd no longer have any authority at work. If she even still had a job, that is.

"Oh, they'll keep you all right. They have no choice. I'm still the boss, even though I'll be suspended until there's an actual verdict. If I were to be convicted, then they'd have cause to fire me, but not before. Anyway, Darla has been very supportive of me through this whole thing. She'll do whatever I ask of her if she thinks it will help."

The problem was, Darla couldn't help *me* because she didn't know my real role at NUTEC, and I was still unwilling to have anyone there told the truth about that. Still, there was no point in adding to Mrs. Thompson's worry at the moment. I said nothing and hoped that something would happen to clear my best friend's mother very soon.

CHAPTER ELEVEN

I'd barely walked into the kitchen at my place when I heard a crash from the living room. Since I knew I was home alone, it scared me half to death until I saw the black streak tear down the hall and disappear under the table behind me.

"What have you done?" I asked, leaning down and shaking my head. Whatever it was, it sure didn't sound like something Mom was going to be happy about.

Ernie looked back at me, wild-eyed and terrified. I could almost see his little kitty heart pounding.

"Oh, you're all right," I told him. "No need to put on a big show just to try to get out of trouble." Then it occurred to me that maybe something had fallen *on* him and he could be hurt.

"C'mere," I whispered softly, holding my hand out toward him. "It's okay, don't be scared."

Ernie showed no sign of regaining his courage right then, and I figured trying to grab him would only lead to more trouble. Besides, he wasn't bleeding or anything, so chances were good he'd only frightened himself. Maybe, I thought, that will be a deterrent to future bad behaviour.

I went to the living room to inspect the damage and found that he'd knocked over a ceramic peacock that my dad's sister, Aunt Denise, had made. It was in dozens of pieces. I groaned inwardly and started gathering it up. This was bound to be the end of the line for Ernie. No way was Mom going to let me keep him another day.

You'd almost think, with all the havoc he'd created, that would have been a relief, but oddly enough, it wasn't. I was getting more and more fond of the little guy. Besides, I didn't want to let Mr. Stanley down.

There wasn't much I could do about it, though I had a moment of temptation when I thought of cleaning it up and not saying anything. It was possible that Mom might not notice for a while. (Dad might *never* notice, being a guy and all, so it was only Mom I had to worry about.) I dismissed the idea quickly, though, because it's been my experience that I'm not what you'd call lucky with that sort of situation. Somehow, I knew, it would come back and cause me grief.

I gathered up all the brightly coloured chunks of ceramic and carried them to the kitchen, where I bagged them in a couple of paper bags and then a plastic one, which I tied. That went into the garbage in the porch, and I grabbed the broom and dustpan to go sweep up the rest. Before I could get there, though, the phone rang.

"Hello?" The call display said unknown number. Probably a telemarketer.

"Hey! You're home."

"Greg!" My heart leapt with excitement and happiness to hear his voice on the other end.

"Yeah. I called earlier and your mom said you were at work."

"Mmhmm. I started a new job today, at NUTEC." I hesitated and then filled him in as quickly as I could on the whole story.

"There's *no* danger," I emphasized as I wrapped it up. Greg has a bit of a problem when he thinks I'm doing things that could get me hurt or killed. I guess boyfriends tend to be like that.

"Be really careful anyway," he said quietly. "If the stolen software is worth millions, well, there are people who would do almost anything to make sure they don't lose that kind of money."

"Don't worry. I'll be careful," I said. "Anyway, when are you coming home?"

"Hopefully in a couple more days." He made this funny sound then, like a he was clearing his throat and groaning at the same time. "I miss you like crazy, Shelby."

"Me too. I mean, I miss *you*. I can't wait to see you." I sighed and added, "I wish you were coming home now."

"I do too, in a way, but in another way I'm glad we're here. This trip has been really good for Dad. I think it's the closest he's been to happy since my mom died."

Greg's mother died in a fire two years ago, the summer before he and his dad moved to Little River. His father, Dr. Taylor, is a really nice guy, but you can always see this sadness in him, even behind laughter. I was happy to hear that the trip was doing him so much good.

"He's so much more like his old self, relaxed and everything," Greg went on. "I've gotten used to seeing a hint of strain in him, no matter how hard he tries to hide it. It's great to see him like this."

"I'm really glad to hear it, Greg," I said. "I like your dad a lot."

"That's one of the many things I admire about you," Greg said softly. "You always think of others."

"Well, I'm pretty much a saint," I said lightly, embarrassed by the compliment.

"I'm not sure I'd go quite that far," he said. "Anyway, I'd better get going. I'll try to call you again when I know for sure what day we're leaving to come home."

"Okay." I swallowed hard, trying not to feel sad. "I'm awful glad you called."

"Me too. Bye."

"Bye," I said. I held the phone for a couple of seconds until I heard the click, just in case. Then I slowly put the receiver back on the cradle and took a deep breath.

I told myself that it would be ridiculous to cry, but I knew I was on the verge anyway. A sharp pang of loneliness jabbed me right in the stomach and made it kind of hard to breathe properly.

Tears were threatening to form when I felt something land in my lap, purring loudly.

"Ernie!" I said, startled. "What are you doing?"

In answer, he rubbed his face against my arm a few times, kneaded me like a lump of dough, and then curled into a ball and made himself good and comfortable. He continued to hum like a little motor and gland me with the side of his face. It was a welcome distraction, and I found myself patting him and scratching his chin gently, which made him purr even louder.

"You're not such a bad guy, are you?" I said. "I'm not sure how we're going to get you out of the spot you're in over the broken peacock, but I'll see what I can do. Mom might give you one more chance, but you've got to start behaving a bit better."

I was right in the middle of my speech when he suddenly jumped down and walked off. It occurred to me that he'd sensed my mood and come to comfort me, then left when he figured the job was done. That made me really determined to somehow persuade Mom to let him off this time.

Turned out, though, that there was no persuading needed. When they got home I explained what had happened and begged Mom not to evict the poor little guy.

"Well, now, it *was* just an accident," Mom said. "We'll just put anything valuable out of harm's way while he's here."

While Dad went off to make himself a snack, she patted Ernie and told him it was okay. Her reaction was nothing like what I'd expected, and I told her I was surprised how well she'd taken it.

"There are some things that are, uh, easier to part with than others," she whispered, winking at me. "In fact, do you think you can get him to knock over the ceramic elephant in my sewing room, too?"

"Mom!" I was shocked in spite of my relief. "Aunt Denise made those things for you!"

"Yes," she said sadly, "I know. That's why they've been on display all this time."

Then she scooped Ernie up and kissed him on the forehead. He did *not* look impressed.

CHAPTER TWELVE

I was nervous going to NUTEC the next morning. It was impossible to predict what kind of reaction there'd be to Mrs. Thompson's arrest, and I was afraid if someone said the wrong thing I might give myself away. I know it's human nature to joke about things that make us uncomfortable, but if anyone made a crack about my best friend's mother, I didn't trust myself to remain neutral.

It was a relief, therefore, to find that the mood at the office was serious and concerned.

Janine looked outright angry, and she turned toward me as soon as I crossed the threshold and said, "Marion was arrested!" The look on her face was almost accusing, like it was my fault that this terrible thing had happened.

It took me a second or two to realize that Marion was Mrs. Thompson, though I must have heard her first name at some time in the past — likely without it really registering. Having made the connection, I stood there silently, not knowing if I should say anything. I couldn't pretend I knew nothing about it, but commenting would be likely to give me away. Fortunately, others were arriving just then and they all had something to say about the new development.

"You *can't* be serious," Stuart Yaeger said while his wife shook her head disbelievingly. Apparently they were hearing the news for the first time. "They actually laid charges?"

"I'm sure she'll be cleared," Darla spoke from the doorway. "The evidence is all circumstantial. In the meantime, the best thing we can all do is focus on our work. That way, when she returns, everything will be running smoothly."

"Maybe there's more than just circumstantial evidence," Debbie Yaeger remarked. "The police must feel that they have a strong case if they've gone this far with it. Who knows, maybe they've learned something new. Has anyone heard anything … like if they've found an eyewitness or something?"

No one had. I would have been surprised if there'd been anyone around in the middle of the night in this particular part of town. I thought Debbie's idea was a bit silly, but maybe she was just trying to make sense of an arrest that went against everything she knew about Mrs. Thompson.

On the other hand, what did *I* honestly know about her?

Lying in bed the night before, thinking and thinking, that exact question had come to me, and the more I thought about it the more I had to admit that I really know very little about Mrs. Thompson. She's my friend's mom, yes, but aside from saying "hi" and answering the usual parent questions (like, where are you girls going and what time will you be back) I never even talk to her.

Well, I figured that the best way to learn a bit about what kind of person she was would be to get the people she works with talking about her. I couldn't come right out and ask if they thought she was capable of committing a crime, but maybe I could come up with something a little less direct. Something that wouldn't make it obvious I was fishing for information. I needed to find some way to get them talking.

Aside from the morning's discussion about the arrest, the day was fairly uneventful. Janine actually did some typing and filing while I continued getting the month's bills ready to go out. She seemed much quieter than the day before, which may have been because she was busier but was more likely because she was absorbed with thoughts of her boss's problems. I thought it was nice that she was so concerned.

When closing time arrived I was hungry, so I decided to grab something to eat before going to see Mr. Stanley. I wanted to drop off the book he'd asked for, which I'd picked up at the library at lunchtime. I was going to get a six-inch sub, but then I thought of the hospital food and instead ordered a foot-long — steak and mushroom with lots of veggies. I hurried to the hospital and got to his room while it was still nice and warm.

"Bless your heart," he said half a dozen times, happily munching down his half. "Now *this* is food!" His own meal, just like the day before, sat almost untouched beside a cup of melting ice chips.

After we'd eaten, we talked about Ernie (there seemed no need to mention the accident with the peacock), then I gave him *Seventeen*, fetched his glasses from the bed stand, and said I'd be by again the next day.

My next stop was Betts's place, and after such a fruitless day I dreaded going there. Mrs. Thompson seemed happy to see me, though, and in slightly better spirits than the day before.

"I have a copy of the file here, just like I promised. And you know, Betts has so much confidence in you that it's starting to be contagious. She tells me you've solved other crimes in the most amazing way, and, why, I suppose some people just have a certain knack for that sort of thing. So, let me get that file from the other room and you can have a look at it."

I took it from her feeling like a total fraud. I've been lucky and happened on to some solutions in the past, it's true, but I was getting nowhere with this, and I hated to see her so hopeful when I was probably going to let her down.

"I'll take this home and look at it where I can concentrate," I said after I'd glanced through it quickly. While I'd flipped pages, she'd stood beside me with an expectant air, like I might, at any minute, leap to my feet, shout "Aha!" and solve the whole thing.

"Oh, well, okay." She sounded disappointed but covered it with an overly bright smile.

"You know, I really can't promise anything," I said, feeling like a criminal myself.

"Of course not, dear. You just do your best. I'm sure it will all be fine in the long run."

Betts walked part of the way home with me. "You must have *some* ideas," she said.

"The thing is, Betts, I don't know any of these people. It's hard when I have no background or anything to go on. I mean, I can't even tell if someone is doing anything unusual or out of character."

"I see what you mean," she agreed, nodding, but then shrugged it off. "You'll still figure it out, though. I know you will. You *have* to."

"I'll sure try," I said, pushing down feelings of hopelessness. Changing the subject, I asked her how things were with her and her boyfriend, Derek.

"Okay, I guess." She shrugged.

"He knows you're home, right?"

"Yeah. I called him Saturday, after you left. He's supposed to come over tonight."

Something didn't seem quite right about that. If he hadn't seen her for two weeks before she called, why was he taking until Tuesday to see her?

"Was everything okay with you two before you went away? Uh, I mean..."

She laughed. "Before we *pretended* to go away. I know, it's weird. My mom was kind of in a state and some of the ideas she came up with then weren't what you'd call totally sane."

"I guess anyone would be pretty upset over something like that and not thinking exactly straight."

"I guess. It was awful, though, stuck in the house, not allowed to go anywhere or call anyone."

"I'm surprised your mom answered the door the day I saw her and went over to your place."

"That's only because I saw you and I told her if she didn't let you in I was going to."

"Right. Well, anyway, like I was asking, were things okay with you and Derek the last time you saw him?"

"I suppose. But you know, it's not the same as it was before. I'm thinking it might be time to dump him."

"What do you mean, it's not the same? What's changed?"

She stopped walking and turned to face me. "He's, like, all wrapped up in other things all the time. When we started going out everything was great. He used to pay a lot of attention to me. Now there's hardly any, I dunno exactly, romance, maybe. No, it's more like excitement. That's just not there anymore."

"You still like him, though, don't you?"

"Yeah, I like him. I'm just not sure if it's *that way* now." She laughed and shook her head. "This probably isn't the best time for me to make this kind of decision. Anyway, I'm starting to sound like some stuck-up, high-maintenance girlfriend, which I don't really think I am."

"No, you're not," I agreed. And she isn't. She just never seems to really know what she wants, and every relationship ends like this — with a note of dissatisfaction. Derek had outlasted all previous boyfriends, though, and I'd thought she was quite happy with him. They'd broken up once before, around my birthday, which was on June 11, but that hadn't lasted twenty-four hours.

On a selfish note, it was great for me, too, because Greg and I double-dated with them sometimes. You know how it is when you have a best friend and a boyfriend and you want to spend time with both of them but you can't always work it out, and then someone feels left out? That's never been a problem since she's been seeing Derek.

We talked for a few more minutes and she said she was going to wait for a few weeks to see how things went before making a decision. She left for her place then, and I hurried home to have a good look at the file.

Chapter Thirteen

There wasn't much in the file that was new information to me. Mainly, the evidence repeated the things I'd already been told, like that the window was broken from the inside to make it look like someone had come in that way and that Mrs. Thompson was the only one (at that time) who had keys to get into the offices, as well as the only one who had the safe combination.

I dialled the Thompsons' phone number. It rang three times.

"Hello, Mrs. Thompson?"

"Yes, dear. Did you want Betts?"

"No, actually, I wanted to ask you something."

"Oh. Well, go ahead."

"Last summer, when you went on holidays, someone must have had the keys, right?"

"Yes. Darla would have had them, just as she does this year. She always fills in for me."

"What's to have prevented her from making a second set?"

"Oh, I see where you're going with this. No, I'm afraid that won't work. You see, we have the main lock changed every three months for security reasons. The locks are always changed within a week of my return from holidays. On top of that, they would have been changed again several times since then. The keys in use right now were almost brand new when the robbery occurred and no one other than myself had them at any time."

"You never leave them anywhere that one of your staff could just pick them up casually and go somewhere quickly to have a copy cut?"

"Absolutely not. I know this probably doesn't help me, but that's one thing I'm particularly careful about. Those keys are on my person all day. In fact, I wear them on a key belt. First thing I do every morning is clip them on to that. For someone to get a copy, why, they'd have to take me along, too."

"Do you keep a spare set somewhere that someone might have discovered?"

"There *is* a spare set, but no one knows where it's kept, and accessing it without me finding out about it would be almost impossible. It's not even kept at the office."

"Okay, well, I just thought I'd check on the whole key thing." I did my best to keep my voice neutral, but I admit I was feeling pretty disappointed. I'd thought I'd hit on something important that might help clear Mrs. Thompson, but it was more likely to help the prosecution!

"What about the safe combination?" I almost didn't want to ask, in case it further strengthened the case against her. Still, I had to know.

"The safe combination … oh, I guess you want to know if someone else has it while I'm away, and so forth. Well, actually, no. When I'm on holidays, anything that needs to be locked up is kept in Darla's filing cabinet in a small, fireproof lockbox. It's not nearly as secure, but in spite of the measures we take to protect our data, theft isn't really all that usual. A person would have to know what was in development and when it was functional before they'd know which disks would be worth stealing."

"What if you *forgot* the combination to the safe, or…?" I hesitated, not really wanting to say what I'd been thinking.

"I keel over and die?" she laughed, finishing the sentence for me. "I have it written down, in my safety deposit box at the bank, where I keep my important documents."

"Are the disks password protected?" I felt more discouraged by the minute and almost didn't want to ask any more questions. Everything she'd told me so far only made her look guilty.

"Of course. But there's no code or password that can't be broken if you have the time and know-how. Or even the right program."

"Okay." I couldn't think of anything else, and anyway, as I've said, her answers weren't helping. "Well, thanks. I'll call back if I need to know anything else."

"You do that, dear."

I dropped the phone back into the cradle feeling less hopeful than ever, but I forced myself to open the file again. A manila envelope on the bottom of the stack of papers caught my eye and I pulled it out and opened it.

Inside were eight-by-ten pictures of the conference room, all taken on the day of the robbery. I slid them out and spread them across the kitchen table, looking at them as if the culprit might suddenly materialize there.

I noticed the fridge right away, because it's not normally in the conference room. It looked very much out of place, sitting between the water cooler and the safe. The police had even taken a couple of shots of it with the doors open. The exciting contents consisted of a small milk carton, coffee cream, a couple of plastic containers holding unidentified foods, and a plastic bag with three or four apples in it. The freezer was empty.

The conference table and filing cabinets had been photographed too, even though the table was bare except for the stone eagle and the filing cabinets appeared to be locked and untouched. The books I'd seen on top of them seemed undisturbed. I noticed that there was a big fern and a spider plant on the cabinets, sitting at opposite ends. The fern looked like the one in Darla's office, and the spider plant, if I was right, was now in the reception area, hanging in the corner.

The window had been photographed from a number of angles, but there wasn't really much to see aside from the fact that it was broken.

There was a picture that puzzled me for a few moments — a big dark blotch on the carpet. Then I remembered Janine telling me that either the fridge or water cooler had leaked and they'd had to call in a repairman. I tossed that picture aside without wasting any more time on it.

The shots I spent the most time looking at were those of the safe. I'm not sure why I stared at those pictures so long, since they weren't likely to tell me anything. The big heavy door on the front of it hung open, and it was easy to see that the thief had been selective in what he or she had taken. Small stacks of envelopes and plastic cases holding computer disks sat in it practically undisturbed.

I closed my eyes and visualized the room, the long row of filing cabinets, the corner where the safe sat, the window, the desk, the water cooler, the table. I could almost imagine myself in there, walking around, getting the feel of the place.

It didn't help.

After that, I spent a good hour flipping through page after page of statements from the staff. Basically, they all said the same thing — they didn't know anything and hadn't been involved. I drew each person's statement out of the pile one by one and read them carefully, beginning with Joey's.

No, he had no knowledge of the robbery. He'd been home at the time it occurred. No witnesses to his whereabouts. No idea as to who could have done it. I was struck by the totally disinterested tone of his answers and wondered how someone could spend all that time developing a program and then be so complacent about its loss.

The Yaegers said they'd been at home all night and had turned in early after watching their favourite movie — a copy of *Dead Poets Society*, which they owned. Hard to prove or disprove, I thought, unless they'd left the house and someone had seen them. Neither claimed to know anything about the theft and both agreed that there was no one they would suspect among the staff at NUTEC.

Angi's statement seemed to border on insolence in places. She denied any involvement and said she'd been with "a friend" at the time the crime was taking place but refused to give a name. She also went on record that none of her co-workers were brave enough to commit a crime, which I thought was a strange way of saying she didn't think anyone at work had done it.

Darla, James, and Janine had been quite formal with their answers, responding briefly to each question in a simple, straightforward manner. All three claimed they'd been with family members, Darla and James with their spouses, and Janine with her sister, whom she went out of her way to describe as a highly trustworthy person. I smiled at that, since I'd previously heard Janine call her sister a backstabbing lowlife. I don't suppose that's something you'd want to say to the police about the person who was your alibi, though.

The last statement I looked at was Carol's, and it was a bit different from the others. The main thing that stood out was *how* she answered the questions. Although she didn't actually claim to know anything, her answers were vague and worded in a way that made it look like she was hiding something. It seemed pretty deliberate, and I figured she was using the robbery to get attention for herself in any way she could. As for an alibi, she said she'd been taking care of a neighbour. Apparently, she has a second job two nights a week, staying with an elderly woman. It looked like a solid alibi on the surface, but she'd admitted that the old woman had been in bed asleep from nine-thirty on, which meant she could have left and returned without anyone knowing. Bleary-eyed, I put everything back into the file, then showered, brushed my teeth, and got ready for bed. It was barely ten o'clock by then, but I was bushed.

I crawled in, turned my lamp on, and picked up *Nobody's Child* by Marsha Forchuk Skrypuch, the awesome novel I'd started recently. Before long I realized I was reading the same paragraph over and over without taking anything in, so I gave up and switched off the light. Just as I was falling asleep, I felt a thud as Ernie landed on the bed beside me.

Chapter Fourteen

"That woman is going to drive me crazy," Janine hissed at me the next morning, when Carol once again arrived late and managed to turn her tardiness into a reason to give Janine a hard time. "Thank goodness she doesn't spend much time out here."

I was about to say something consoling when Debbie spoke from the doorway of the office she shared with Stuart.

"Janine, could you take down a letter for me?"

"Sure, Deb. Shelby, would you get the phone if it rings while I'm not at my desk? Just do like I showed you if you need to send a call through to anyone's office. Otherwise, take down messages and I'll get to them when I'm done."

I nodded and slid into her seat, feeling kind of important in the real receptionist's chair. I yawned and stretched my arms over my head and then examined my nails. I'm afraid they needed a lot more work than Janine's.

Just then, the phone rang, nearly making me jump off my chair. I picked it up and said, "Good morning, NUTEC, may I help you?" as I'd heard Janine do.

"Stuart Yaeger, please."

"Certainly, sir. May I tell him who's calling?"

"Bryan Balanski from Dymelle Enterprises."

I pushed the button on the phone that would put the caller on hold while I rang Stuart's desk.

"Yes, Mr. Yaeger?" I said, trying to sound professional. "A Mr. Balanski is calling for you from Dymelle Enterprises."

"Who? Oh, yeah. Uh, okay, put him through."

I transferred the call, wishing I had some way of listening in on the conversation. I found myself staring at the light on the phone, as if knowing how long they spoke would tell me anything.

"Lost in thought?"

Startled for the second time, I found myself guiltily facing James, while warmth spread up my neck and across my cheeks.

"Nickel for your thoughts," he said, smiling.

"I thought it was a penny," I said. I wondered how flustered and red-faced I looked.

"Inflation. Anyway, where's Janine?"

"Taking dictation from Mrs. Yaeger."

"Ah, well, when she gets back, tell her I'd like a few moments of her time."

"Is there anything I could help you with?"

"Thanks, but I don't think so. You could tell her, though, that I'd like a printout of the activities of these accounts for the past six months." He handed me a slip of paper with a list of names written on it.

"I'll let her know as soon as she gets back," I said, hoping I sounded efficient.

"Great then." He turned and walked back to his office, passing Carol in the hallway as he went.

"Where's Janine?" she asked, lumbering up to the desk.

"Taking dictation."

"Well, I need her for a minute." She looked at me angrily, as though I'd deliberately sent Janine off in order to inconvenience her.

"I'm sure she won't be much longer," I said.

"The copier needs toner." Her tone implied that once I understood the importance of her request, I'd hurry up and do something about it.

"She should be back any moment."

"I can't make copies without toner!" Carol said, her voice rising. "I have to get my work done, you know."

"Maybe I can help." I stood, intending to go with her to the copy room, but she became visibly upset by the suggestion.

"No, you can't! Only Janine is trained for that."

"Okay, well..." My words trailed off in relief as I saw Janine coming back down the hall.

"Janine, the toner is empty and this *girl* here wanted to put more in but I wouldn't let her." Carol's voice was so different than it had been the few times I'd heard her speak before that I could scarcely believe it was the same person. All traces of her usual blustery aggression were gone, replaced with a whining, pleading sound.

"I'll get it, just relax," Janine said. She disappeared back down the hall with Carol on her heels and came back alone a couple of minutes later.

"She dumped the toner powder in the wrong place once, and we had to service the machine, so now I always do it," she explained to me as she slid into the chair I'd vacated for her. "She gets pretty freaked out if she can't get her copying done, though she's slower'n a snail at it anyway."

"She acts really different when she needs help," I observed.

"Yeah. I think it panics her when she can't do her work, because she hasn't been able to hold on to jobs in the past. Marion insisted when she came that we were going to give her an honest chance, since she's not very employable. I'd say we've done that all right. And it's not really all that bad since she mostly keeps to herself and does her copying and shredding and stuff."

"Does she shred things that are related to new programs being developed?" I asked.

"Yeah, I guess. Whatever they've printed out that they no longer want, and anything that's confidential — like stuff they might print for presentations. After their meetings they collect up all the copies and send them for shredding right away."

"But the details, the actual codes wouldn't be on anything they'd show at a meeting," I said, thinking out loud. "They'd only present information on what a program did."

"Whatever." Janine gave me a strange look. "You sure ask about weird things. Who cares *what* Carol's in there shredding, as long as she's not out here bothering us."

"You're right," I said quickly. It was clearly time to change the subject. "So, are you taking any holidays this summer?"

"I already took my vacation the end of June," she sighed. "I won't have any more time off until Christmas, though at least there are a few long weekends between now and then."

"Oh!" I jumped up suddenly, which made her start in her seat. "I almost forgot. James, uh, Mr. Rankin wants you to take him the records of these accounts, going back for six months." I passed her the paper he'd handed me.

"Okay." She took the slip and glanced at it, then started typing to bring up the files. However disorganized she seemed, I had to admit she was fast on the computer. In just a few moments she'd sent all the records he'd asked for to the printer and it was zipping and whirring as it spewed out pages. She had me take them to his office when they were ready.

"Well, thanks, but I really need to see Janine for a minute," he said, taking them from me. "Tell her I have questions I need answers to on a few of the billing codes so that I can set these up properly in the tax accounts."

I gave her the message and took over the phone once again while she went off to give him the information he needed.

I was turning the Rolodex on the desk, reading through the names without any real idea of what I expected to find there, when the main door opened and a policeman stepped into the reception area.

"Officer Doucet!" I'd recently had some dealings with him when a friend disappeared. He'd been pretty decent to me — took me seriously and even came by to congratulate me when I'd figured out what was going on. Most importantly, he hadn't treated me like a kid.

"Miss Bel ... uh ... I want to say Bellflower but that's not right, is it?"

"Belgarden. Shelby Belgarden."

"Yes, that's it — Belgarden." He laughed a little at that, probably realizing it sounded silly for him to be confirming my own name for me. "Are you working here?"

"Uh-huh, I just started this week."

"Then you weren't working here with the robbery took place. Or, maybe you haven't heard anything about it."

"I've heard about it," I said simply. No need to tell him I was supposed to be clearing the person they'd just arrested.

"Well, this is one we won't need any help solving," he said, smiling. "We laid charges yesterday. Pretty open-and-shut case, really."

"As much as purely circumstantial evidence can be," I said. Why couldn't I just keep my mouth closed?

"Sounds like you've heard *all* about it," he said. "And that maybe you don't agree with our conclusions."

"I don't know," I admitted. "It looks bad for her, I guess."

"Ironclad," he said grimly. "It's a shame to see a respected citizen involved in something like this, but the evidence is pretty convincing."

"Have you considered other possibilities?" I asked.

"Sure, we look at everything in an investigation. But the bottom line is usually this: If it looks like a duck and sounds like a duck and walks like a duck, chances are pretty good that it's a duck. No need to create a mystery where there is none."

"What if there was something you'd overlooked because it seemed so cut and dried? What if you're sending an innocent woman to prison?"

"Well, you know, Shelby, we try to avoid locking up innocent folk. That's why we investigate carefully and look at every possible angle."

"So, if someone brought something different to your attention — even if it went against your own conclusions, you'd look into it?"

"Of course." He smiled widely and passed me his card. "In fact, to prove it, here's my card. You come up with something new, you call me. I'll listen."

I tucked the card into my wallet, hoping I'd need it.

Chapter Fifteen

Officer Doucet had spoken to only two people — Darla Rhule and Angi Alexander — while he was at NUTEC. Naturally, this made me very curious, but there was no way I could find out what he'd wanted with them.

I spent a few minutes fantasizing about having fancy equipment like they have in movies. Hidden microphones or surveillance cameras would sure come in handy. I could picture myself playing back a tape and hearing the right bit of information. Nothing obvious, though. You know — the phrase that seems innocent and doesn't mean a thing to anyone else but that the really sharp detective catches and explains the significance of to everyone else as he solves the crime.

I think I might have been getting a bit carried away with myself. Fortunately, the fact that I truly hadn't a clue helped put me back in a more humble frame of mind.

At least there was one good thing that came of Officer Doucet's visit. Before that, I'd been feeling pretty down and hopeless. Nothing was falling into place in my head, and the chance that I'd suddenly stumble onto an answer seemed bleak.

Seeing Officer Doucet again reminded me of how I'd felt exactly the same way in the past, and more than once, too. In spite of that, clues would start to make sense and everything would fall together like a big jigsaw puzzle. That helped me a lot because I got a bit of confidence back. All I needed was to actually have the solution come to me.

Angi came out of her office not long after Officer Doucet left. She came over to the reception desk, leaned down, put a finger over her lips for a few seconds, and then whispered, "Is the copper gone?"

"Yeah, the coast is clear," I whispered back.

"I thought they had me this time for sure," she said, expelling her breath in a way that made her cheeks puff out. "I guess I'm just too smart for them after all."

"So, you admit your guilt," I said. "How do you know I won't turn you in?"

"I'll deny it," she said with a wink. "You got nothin' on me."

I laughed.

"Anyway, now that I've given them the slip, there's something else I need."

I waited while she made a show of looking around, like someone might be hidden in the corner listening. "Magenta," she hissed at last.

"Magenta?"

"Ink. For my printer. I'm out and I happen to know that Janine keeps an extra one in her bottom desk drawer. You get it for me, I'll slip you a mint, and it will be our little secret. You can be bought for a mint, can't you?"

"Is it chocolate-coated?" I asked.

"Yeah."

"Then we have a deal." I opened the drawer and found the right colour among a bunch of ink cartridges. She took it, looked it over, winked again, and reached into her pocket. She produced a small brown paper bag, like a miniature lunch sack.

"Here you go," she said, passing me a plain white Scotch mint.

"Hey! This isn't chocolate-coated," I protested.

"You just want to be thankful it's not covered in lint," she laughed. Then she was gone back to her office.

I popped the mint into my mouth just in time for the phone to ring. Even though I pushed it into one cheek with my tongue before answering, my words weren't quite clear.

"I can't hear what you're saying. Is this NUTEC?" a woman's voice asked. She sounded annoyed.

"Yes, ma'am," I said, letting the mint drop with a sticky plop into the palm of my hand.

"I need to speak to Marion Thompson," she said.

"Uh, Mrs. Thompson is on holidays," I said. "Would you like to speak to the person who's filling in for her?"

"No," she said without hesitation. "When will Mrs. Thompson be back from holidays?"

"I'm not exactly sure."

"Well, approximately." She sounded pretty exasperated.

"I'm sorry, but I really don't know, ma'am." I was about to ask if there was a message I could pass on but before I could say anything further there was a click and the dial tone began to hum in my ear. I sat the phone back in the cradle.

"How do you stand impatient or unreasonable people?" I asked Janine, who arrived back from James's office just then.

She shrugged. "Doesn't usually bother me, though once in a while I'd like to give someone a piece of my mind. Mostly, I just … hey, what's that in your hand?"

"Oh, a mint." I stuck it back in my mouth and looked for a tissue to wipe my hand.

"Looks like one of Angi's mints," she said, eyes narrowing. "Okay, what did you give her?"

"Ink," I admitted, feeling like a kid confessing to cookie theft.

"Well, go wash your hands, for goodness' sake. And try not to be bribed so easily the next time. I always get a mint *and* something else, like this." She pulled open a desk drawer and pulled out a cute little caricature sketch of herself painting her nails.

"There was supposed to be chocolate," I said lamely.

"Second lesson." Janine shook her head sadly, as though there was little hope for me. "Never give up the merchandise until *after* you get your payoff. That Angi can't be trusted. She'll promise you Belgian truffles and end up giving you Hershey's kisses."

"So I found out." I went to wash up, all the while thinking of how much Greg would like to have a caricature of me. I wondered if another opportunity would present itself, or if I could just ask her to do one for me. Since she'd fibbed about the chocolate, I figured she kind of owed me.

As I was leaving the washroom, I noticed a small plastic watering can on the floor near the sink. I filled it with water and took it with me.

When I got back to the reception area Janine was on the computer playing spider solitaire. I went over and watered the poor, neglected spider plant hanging in the corner. I was picking off some dead leaves when Janine spoke.

"I wish Debbie would take her stupid plant home. She never takes care of it."

"It used to be in the conference room, didn't it?" I asked, thinking of the pictures of the crime scene.

"Mmhmm. Caused a problem, though, because Darla had put a fern in there first. Later on, Debbie brought this one, put it where Darla's plant had been, and moved the fern to another spot. There was an argument over it, and Darla was pretty mad that Debbie had moved her plant. I guess they both wanted the best light for their own plants or something. To tell the truth, I didn't pay much attention. I thought it was a pretty dumb thing to fight about. In the end, they both took them out of there and this is where the spider plant ended up."

I'd been waiting for her to ask how I'd known that the plant had ever been in the conference room, having realized my mistake as soon as the words were out of my mouth. For some reason, and to my relief, that didn't seem to occur to her. I changed the subject quickly, just to be on the safe side.

Janine gave me a few tasks to complete, simple chores that took neither brains nor concentration. It was while I was in the middle of one of these little jobs that a niggling thought started to worm its way up. You know the kind, when you can actually feel a thought or word or idea coming to the surface, and you know it's the answer to some question you've been trying to puzzle through — and then something happens to distract you and you lose it.

In this particular case, what distracted me was Janine knocking over a paper clip holder, scattering what looked to be a thousand of them all over the floor. She claimed that she couldn't pick them up because of her nails, so I got down on my knees and scrounged around the carpet until I'd gotten them all. All that I could see, anyway.

After that, no amount of concentration would stir up whatever idea had been trying to form. I guess something had triggered it, and without whatever that had been, it just wasn't going to happen.

The rest of the day was uneventful, and by the time I'd made my way to see Mr. Stanley and then gone on to Betts's place, I'd forgotten all about the nagging thought that had been trying to come to the surface.

CHAPTER SIXTEEN

"That cat," my mom said as I walked into the kitchen when I finally got home, "is the strangest animal I've ever seen."

"What did he do?" I asked, not at all eager to hear the answer.

"Well, for one thing, he got up on the couch when I was doing the crossword this afternoon, up on the back of the couch to be exact, and then he tried to drape himself on my head."

"On your *head*?" I tried but failed to suppress a giggle.

"On my head. Then, not half an hour later, Julia Pernell stopped by for a visit and he took some kind of fit, positively hurled himself from the room and hid, if you can believe this, behind the toilet of all places. Wouldn't budge an inch until she'd left, and even then

I had to coax him out with a smoked oyster."

"You fed him a smoked oyster?" I wondered but didn't ask whether she'd opened a can especially for him. "Did he like it?"

"I'd say he did, since he almost head-butted a dent in my leg demanding another one. I told him they were too rich for him to be eating a bunch of them but he wouldn't listen."

"So, how many did you end up giving him?" I asked suspiciously.

"Three." At least she looked embarrassed admitting it.

"Uh-huh. Well, if he gets sick, I'm not cleaning it up. I've been good about feeding and brushing him and cleaning his litter, but I can't be held responsible for what other people do."

"I don't think we need to worry. He started to wash up after the last one and then dozed off on your father's recliner. He's been passed out ever since." Mom's face looked all fond and proud talking about him, even before she added, "He's really quite, well, unusual."

"Maybe after Ernie goes back home, we could get a pet," I said. It seemed like the best possible time to approach the subject.

"Maybe," was all she said in reply. "Ernie is a kind of unusual name for a cat. I wonder how he came to be called that."

"I dunno, I'll ask Mr. Stanley tomorrow when I go to the hospital."

"You go to see him every day?" Mom looked surprised.

"Yeah. He doesn't have many visitors — mostly just his daughter when she can find time to go there. She works and has kids so it's kind of hard for her."

"Well, that's really sweet of you, dear. I'm sure it means a lot to him. Time can go by pretty slowly when you're in the hospital. There's so little to do, the high-lights of the day are meals, and they're not always what you'd call great."

"That reminds me — I wanted to take him some fruit and other snacks. He doesn't care too much for the food, and from what I've seen of it, I really don't blame him. Can you help me make up a nice basket?"

Of course Mom agreed to that. She's a bit of a do-gooder, so she loves any chance she gets to do something nice for someone, whether she knows them or not.

She happened to have a wicker basket that was per-fect for what I wanted, so a quick trip to the grocery store was all we needed. Then she arranged the stuff — pears, apples, oranges, bananas, kiwi, grapes, a few kinds of chocolate, wafers, and fancy crackers. It looked beautiful when she was finished and had done it all up in cellophane and ribbon.

"I'll pick you up after work tomorrow and drop you off at the hospital with it, if you like," Mom offered.

"That'd be perfect — thanks!"

"No problem. Oh, it almost slipped my mind. Greg called a while ago. He left a number if you want to call him back."

"Of course I do! Where is it?"

"In the kitchen, on the fridge. I put it under the frog magnet."

I ran to the kitchen and snatched the number out from under the magnet and punched it into the dial pad. I was so excited to be calling him that I had to do it three times before I got it right.

"Shelby, I feared you had forsaken me," Greg said, by way of answering the phone.

"I take it they have call display," I giggled.

"Perhaps they do, or perhaps my loneliness has sharpened my senses and heightened my…"

"I miss you too," I sighed. "A lot."

"Yeah, well, that's what I was *trying* to say when you so rudely cut me off. I'll have you know that I was even going to work in the word *bereft*."

"Good word," I said. "Were you going to say how you were all bereft without me, or what?"

"Well, you've ruined it now, so I guess you'll just never know, will you?"

"I guess not," I said, strangely unperturbed by the loss. "So, are you guys still having a good time? And has your dad decided anything about when you're coming home?"

"Yes and no. We're having a good time, except for the one of us who's bereft, and even he is managing to put on a brave front. And no, nothing definite about the return trip, but I suspect we'll likely be on the road by Monday or Tuesday."

"So you'll be home early next week, probably?" It was Wednesday, and I counted the days on my fingers. Six or seven more days! It seemed so far away.

"Probably. But he could just as easily decide to stay for the rest of the month. I'm just guessing."

"I'm not even going to let myself think about that," I insisted. "Talk about something else!"

"Uh, okay. How's the investigation going? Any headway?"

"Not yet. I just can't seem to get anything to come together in my head. Honestly, the closest thing I have to a clue is that there were a couple of plants in the room when the robbery happened."

"And they're not there now?"

"No. They were moved later on. But it's not as though they could have anything to do with the robbery anyway," I sighed. "I wish you were home. Missing you is probably affecting my ability to think straight."

"So, you find that your thinking is muddled and out of focus when I'm not there to influence you?"

"Yeah, sure. That's exactly what I said, all right." I waited for him to make a quick comeback, but there was nothing but silence on the other end of the line. It lasted for nearly half a minute.

"Boy, would I ever like to kiss you right now," he said suddenly. His voice was all husky, and it made me feel weak in the knees and stomach.

"I don't find this is helping," I said when I could finally get some words out. "It's hard enough being apart without you going and saying stuff like that."

He agreed, so we wrapped it up and said good-night. I looked at the phone for a long minute before setting it back in the cradle. I thought of how I'd done the sensible thing instead of letting the conversation get all sloppy and sad. We'd only have ended up feeling way worse.

I could cheerfully have kicked myself.

CHAPTER SEVENTEEN

"We are going to be killed *for sure* this time."

This was Janine's greeting remark to me the next morning when I arrived for work. I must say that I really prefer a simple good morning.

"What have we done that demands our execution?" I inquired, following her lead in forfeiting the standard hello.

"We totally forgot to do up the July quote summaries. Now Darla is waiting for them and they're not even started." She dropped her head between both hands and lamented, "We're dead."

"How long will it take to do up these, uh, summaries that our lives apparently depend on?" I asked. I didn't bother pointing out that *we* hadn't forgotten to do them — *she* had forgotten to do them. It would have been hard for me to forget them, since I'd never even heard of them in the first place.

"Hours and hours. Most of the day, probably, depending on how many interruptions there are. And Darla just buzzed me for them."

"Did you tell her they're not done?"

"Are you crazy?" Janine looked at me as though I'd just escaped from a mental institution. "Of course not. She'd have a fit."

"Don't you think she might notice when you don't take them to her?"

"I was going to think of some reason to stall. Like, tell her the printer is acting up or something, and that they're ready but I can't print them out yet."

"Don't they all have printers in their own offices?" I asked, thinking of how Angi had finagled an ink cartridge out of me for a plain old boring mint.

"Yeah, but they're not connected to my computer."

"But if you lie about it, aren't you running the risk that she'll just tell you to load the information on a disk and she'll print it herself?" I knew from experience that lies have a way of turning on you. Besides, Darla didn't strike me as all that fierce.

"Oh, I don't know," Janine moaned pitifully. "I just don't know what to do."

"How about just telling her the truth — that you forgot and you'll get them done as quickly as possible?"

"The *truth*?" She sounded incredulous. "Do you think that might work?"

"I'll tell her if you want," I said. "The sooner that's over with the better. Then we can actually start doing them."

"Okay," she looked doubtful. "I hope she doesn't bite your head off."

I figured she was overreacting, but Darla was far from happy at the news once I'd delivered my message.

"Janine knows those are to be done at the start of every month without fail. There's no excuse for her not having them ready."

"It probably slipped her mind because she was busy training me and all," I said. I felt no relief at all that she was putting the blame fully on Janine, even though it *was* her fault.

"I'm sure she remembered to do her nails and play with that mop of hair and make personal phone calls," Darla said shortly. "Anyway, that's neither here nor there. Tell her I want them by the end of the day and no excuses. I can't run a business if things aren't done properly and on time."

"Yes, ma'am." I was only too glad to get out of there and go back to the reception area. I noticed, as I passed the offices along the way, that the Yaegers' door was open and they weren't in yet. The temptation to just take a quick peek in there was strong, but picturing what would happen if I got caught stopped me.

It was just as well, since they arrived only seconds after I'd passed Darla's message on to Janine. With barely a nod in our direction they headed down the hall, neither of them looking overly happy.

"Trouble in paradise," Janine whispered. "They don't fight often but when they do anyone could tell just looking at them. I bet it's about a baby."

"A *baby*?"

"They've been trying to start a family for years, but with no luck. So every once in a while Debbie gets on this kick that she wants to adopt a foreign kid from, I dunno exactly, a Third World country or something. Only Stuart doesn't want to. He gives her all these excuses, but she thinks it's really because it's expensive and he tends to be kind of tight with money."

"How do you know all this?" I asked, curious.

"Oh, Debbie and I have had some long heart-to-hearts over lunch. She needs someone to talk to, because she has no family around here and she and Stuart don't socialize enough for her to have close friends. Little River is originally Stuart's home, not hers."

"Where's she from?"

"Pickering, Ontario. But her mother was the last person left there from her family, and she moved to a retirement community somewhere near Sudbury, in Northern Ontario. Elliot Lake, I think. Anyway, now

VALERIE SHERRARD

Debbie feels kind of adrift, like her background is all wiped out or something. She told me that makes her want a baby even more, though I can't quite understand what one thing has to do with the other."

"Do they know if there's some reason they haven't been able to have a baby of their own?" I felt kind of creepy asking something that personal about people I hardly knew, but it had occurred to me that there were medical procedures available for couples in that situation, and some of them could be pretty expensive. Of course, I had no way of knowing whether or not Debbie would steal in order to get the money for something like that, but it did sound as though she was getting desperate to have a family.

"I don't really know. I got the impression that they were still trying, though." Janine seemed to have tired of this particular conversation, since she reached into her purse and drew out her manicure kit, a small burgundy case that held clippers, a tiny pair of scissors, a nail file, emery boards, and whatever those things are called that push back cuticles.

"Uh, Janine, did you want me to start on those summaries?" I asked.

"The summaries!" She tossed the kit back into her bulging purse and slapped herself on the forehead. "I can't believe I was going to forget about them again! What is *wrong* with me?"

The phone rang before I could respond to that, which was probably just as well. She answered it, put a call through to Angi's office, and then started tapping on the keyboard. Her fingers flew as she typed, and I was struck once again by how fast and efficient she was when she actually did some work.

While she did that I busied myself with a bit of dusting. There's a cleaning person who comes in on Monday mornings, but the job he does wouldn't earn him any awards, that's for sure. I wiped off the desks and filing cabinets and window ledges in the reception area, then did the lunchroom and conference room. When I'd finished, I stood and surveyed the conference room for a few minutes. While I did that, I pictured the photos from the robbery, willing something to click into place.

Nothing.

CHAPTER EIGHTEEN

At around eleven o'clock, while Janine was working furiously on the summaries (I still had no idea what that meant, and it didn't look as though she intended to fill me in), a couple of men in suits came into the reception area and asked for Darla. Well, actually, they asked for Ms. Rhule.

I was dispatched to let her know they'd arrived, and she told me to escort them into the conference room and make them comfortable. Just how I was supposed to make them comfortable she didn't say. I didn't want to go overboard, so I just offered them a seat and asked if they would like coffee.

"A bottle of club soda for me," the taller of the two said without looking at me.

"I'll have a diet soda. Preferably Pepsi, if you have it," said the other, also without so much as a glance in my direction.

I told them certainly and then dashed back to the reception area and asked Janine if we had a stash of various beverages anywhere. On learning we didn't, I hurried downstairs, outside, and across the street to a nearby convenience store.

All told, it must have taken five minutes for me to deliver their drinks. It was a warm day, too, and I think I looked a little flushed from hurrying, but since they acted like I didn't even exist, I didn't worry about them noticing. I sat the bottles, along with ice-filled glasses, on the table in front of them. They were opening briefcases and getting out folders and notepads and neither thanked me nor even acknowledged that I'd given them anything.

I couldn't help thinking that my mother would have been appalled at their rudeness, but I guess if you're some kind of a bigshot in the business world, you might get the idea that you're too good for common manners. Mom says people like that have gotten a bit too big-feeling.

Anyway, I was about to exit the room when Darla came in. She looked at the drinks and then at me with a sort of questioning expression that was quickly chased off by a smile of approval.

"Can I get anything for you, ma'am?" I asked her.

"Thank you, Shelby, but I'm fine." She stepped forward to greet the men, who both rose and extended hands toward her.

I nearly bumped into Joey on the way back down the hall. He was coming out of Angi's office, talking and walking backwards. I managed to stop in time, but just barely, and I nearly lost my balance in the process.

"Oops, sorry about that," he said, grabbing my arm to steady me. "I should have been watching where I was going, but if you've had any dealings with Angi, you already know it's best never to turn your back on her."

"She did cheat me out of chocolate yesterday," I said solemnly.

"I'm not surprised. That's just like her. If I wasn't working on a project with her right now, I'd stay barricaded in my room with fresh garlic hanging in the doorway."

"It would improve the smell of the place," she commented without looking up from her desk. "He's got this desk his grandfather made for him with secret compartments. I swear, he uses them to hide food until it moulds and rots."

"One time! One time I forgot about a bologna sandwich." Joey lifted his chin and made an indignant sound. "Don't ever make a mistake here, Shelby. You'll never be allowed to live it down."

"I'll try not to," I said. My brain had grabbed on to the mention of a secret compartment, though, and was running it through a few questions. As intriguing as it sounded, I found it did little to offer up any ideas related to the robbery. After all, it wouldn't help a person get into the locked conference room or the safe. You needed keys and codes for those things, not a place you could hide things.

I was suddenly aware of Carol, standing nearby at the copy room door watching Joey and me. She huffed loudly, apparently trying to give us the message that we were disturbing her.

"If you don't mind, this is a place of business," she said angrily, just before she turned and flounced back into her work area.

Joey shook his head mildly, obviously not intending to let her get to him. Angi, on the other hand, either hadn't heard what Carol said or had decided to ignore her completely. She bent back down to something she was working on at her desk.

I thought I'd better get back to work too and returned to the reception area to find Janine looking flustered and angry.

"Is something wrong?" I asked.

"I can't open some of these files," she muttered. "I keep getting stupid prompts for passwords — which this program doesn't even use — and the only way I can get back in is by rebooting the whole system. That seemed to work for a few of them, but there are half a dozen or so that I can't get at no matter what I try."

"I wish I could help," I said, "but my computer knowledge is pretty basic."

She looked at me as though I'd said something brilliant, which I was relatively certain I hadn't. "Of course!" she said, though she seemed to be talking to the air more than to me. "Why didn't I think of that before?"

"Think of what?"

"The geeks. This place is full of computer geniuses. One of them will know what to do."

"Do you want me to ask one of them to help?"

"Okay. Uh, maybe Joey could do it. He can figure anything out."

"I'll see if he can spare a few minutes." I headed back down the hall and tapped on his door.

"Who is it?" he called.

"Shelby."

"Just a sec."

I heard scraping sounds, like something being moved on the floor, only it couldn't have been because the floors are carpet. I waited for what seemed a full two minutes before he told me to come in.

I explained that Janine was having a problem and wanted to know if he might be able to help. He smiled, friendly as ever, and followed me down the hall.

Janine filled him in on what the program was doing and then vacated her chair. Joey plunked down in it and looked puzzled for a moment or two. Then his fingers began to fly on the keyboard and he started talking to himself. Nothing he said made the least bit of sense to me, or to Janine either, if the look on her face was any indication. It was as though he was talking in a totally different language.

I got to wondering if he might break the keyboard, the way he was pounding on the letters. He must ruin a lot of them if that's his normal typing method.

In any case, it seemed he'd just started and then he was getting to his feet. "Should be the very best now," he said.

Janine thanked him with an unmistakable shine in her eyes, though he didn't seem to notice.

CHAPTER NINETEEN

It seemed as though we'd just gone back to work after lunch when I glanced at the clock and saw that it was already almost four in the afternoon.

"How are you doing with the summaries?" I asked Janine, hardly able to believe the day had flown by so quickly.

"Just a couple more," she said, sweeping hair off her forehead with her fingers. "Thank goodness for Joey or I'd really have been sunk."

"He seems like a nice guy," I ventured casually. I was pleased when she took the bait.

"Yeah. Only, he's a bit dense when it comes to women," she said, lowering her voice to a murmur.

"How do you mean?"

"Okay, can you keep a secret?" she asked after a few seconds of silent deliberation. Her voice had dropped to a whisper by then.

"Sure," I said.

"I kind of like him." It was cute how she lowered her eyes and blushed saying this. I wished I could make it so he liked her back.

"Does he know?" I asked.

"No. I mean, he *should* know, but he's managed to miss every hint I've dropped. And I can't do anything too radical like actually ask him out, because, you know, we work together and it would get all weird if he wasn't interested."

"But neither one of you are seeing anyone as far as you know?"

"He dates, I think, but no one really steady. I, on the other hand," she looked embarrassed again, "actually do have a boyfriend. He's a total loser, though. No job, no education, no ambition. I've dumped him like half a dozen times and he keeps coming back and making promises about how he's going to change, but he never keeps them."

"Why do you take him back, then?"

"I dunno. Stupid, I guess. Or a slow learner." She laughed humourlessly. "I guess I get bored or lonely, and then it seems as though Jason is better than nobody."

"There must be *something* good about him," I said, thinking how sad it would be if she said there wasn't.

"Oh, I guess he has a few good points, only I've stopped seeing them. We used to laugh a lot together, but I got tired of his shtick after a while. When we first started going out, I thought he was witty, but I found out pretty fast that it was like a performance — a kind of routine. You can't laugh at the same dumb things over and over."

I knew a few kids at school who were kind of like she was describing. They had some funny lines, but once you'd heard them, that was it. There was nothing new, unless they picked up some fresh material, and then that was just something else for them to overuse.

"The sad thing is," she was continuing, "he's not the first boyfriend I've had who was like that. It's like a pattern for me. If I ever did get to go out with someone like Joey, someone who's got something going for him, I bet I'd just blow it anyway."

"Why would you think that?" I asked, shocked.

"'Cause what would he see in me, honestly? I've got nothing going for me to attract a guy who's smart and has a good job. I'm boring! I probably end up with the Jasons of the world because that's what I deserve. We're suited to each other."

"I can't believe you think that," I said. "You've got all kinds of qualities. In the few days I've been working here, I've seen you do a job that's pretty complicated, handle difficult people, and you still showed me around and trained me for a few things. And you did it all in pretty good humour. Plus, you're pretty."

"What? Nah, my nose is too big."

Now this one I was used to. Betts is constantly complaining about her nose, which she refers to as The Honker. How ridiculous this really is you couldn't appreciate unless you actually saw her nose, which is perfectly normal sized. I can't quite understand why so many of the kids I know seem to believe their noses are bigger than they should be, but it's pretty common, all right. I don't know what kind of mirror they're using, but it must be distorting what they see.

"There's not a thing wrong with your nose," I said truthfully, knowing from experience that I might as well tell it to the desk.

"Oh, no! Not if you're Mr. Potato Head, that is. Anyone else would find it hideous."

"Come on, you can't be serious." I knew she was, though, and I knew this wasn't an argument I could win. She'd have to either settle it for herself someday or go through life believing this ridiculous thing. I couldn't help.

"Shhh, here he comes," she whispered suddenly, turning back to her computer.

Without making it obvious I turned slightly toward the hallway and saw that Joey was indeed headed our way.

"I was bored," he said, dropping a disk on the desk in front of Janine. "So I emailed myself the program you were using after I repaired it. It didn't seem very efficient — I take it that Stuart designed it at some point in time. He tends to go about things in the most impractical ways. Anyway, I modified it so that you can compile your results as you go along, instead of going in and out of files."

He was around the desk by then, standing beside her. "Finish what you're doing here, and I'll install it to override the old program. You can keep this disk as backup if you have any trouble. Just uninstall and reinstall it if there's ever a problem."

Pink tinged Janine's cheeks as she typed in the final details for the last summary and sent it to the printer where a stack of pages already lay. Then she yielded her seat to Joey.

He plunked down and stuck the disk into the drive, pounded on keys for a while, and then turned to her and explained how to work the modified program.

"Hey, thanks a lot, Joey," she said when he was done. She gave him a huge smile.

"No prob. I know how much you hate to actually do any work. Unfortunately, I couldn't come up with something that would do it *for* you, but this will at least cut down on what you have to do."

He strolled back to his office, but only long enough to turn out the lights and pull the door closed. While he was doing that, I whispered to Janine, "Ask if you can take him out for a bite to thank him for doing that for you. That will seem perfectly natural, not like asking him on a real date."

"I can't," she hissed back, but her eyes lit up at the thought.

"C'mon, just do it."

"I don't know if..." She trailed off as Joey approached us again.

"I'm outta here," he said, lifting his hand in a kind of wave-salute combination.

I nudged Janine with my foot, knowing it was hidden from his sight by the desk.

"Uh, Joey," she started, then faltered.

He stopped and turned toward her questioningly. I nudged her harder.

"I was wondering if I could ... you know ... buy you a bite to eat ... for doing that program for me. Just ... you know ... to say thanks?"

"Sure! I'm starved," he said, patting his stomach.

I felt like quite the matchmaker as they left together, Janine looking shy and a bit scared.

Angi and Darla came down the hall a moment later. They seemed surprised to find me alone in the reception area.

"Janine already gone?" Darla asked, pausing at the desk.

"Uh, she's taking Joey for a bite to eat," I said, wondering, even as I spoke, if I should be mentioning it. I worried that it might seem like I was hiding something if she found out later. "He did some computer program for her and she wanted to thank him or something."

"My vote's with 'or something,'" Angi snickered. "She's been after him for ages."

"What do you mean?" Darla asked.

"You've gotta be kidding. You never noticed that Janine is all gone on Joey? She might as well have it tattooed on her forehead. I'm just surprised that she finally hit on him in a way he couldn't miss," Angi said. Her voice sounded mean and amused all at once.

"She wasn't hitting on him," I protested, trying to explain. Darla didn't look impressed.

"Workplace romance is never good," she said. "First thing, someone's fighting or breaking up and you've got two people who don't even speak. One of them would have to go, and it certainly wouldn't be Joey. I'm not having this place negatively affected by personal matters."

I wished I'd minded my own business, but it was too late. The damage was done and there didn't seem to be anything I could do to make it better.

CHAPTER TWENTY

I stepped out into the sunlight feeling terrible about the whole situation I'd just caused. All I'd meant to do was help and cheer Janine up. It was hard to see how my good intentions had turned around so completely and ended up in such a mess.

James and Angi had already gone, and Carol had left the building at the same time I had. Of course, she didn't deign to speak as she walked toward the small parking lot where her car was parked. I stood there, kind of lost in thought, and watched as she drove off in an old blue Sunfire.

Debbie and Stuart came along a moment later, followed almost immediately by Darla, who had returned to her office for something after the unfortunate talk about Janine and Joey. I noticed that the Yaegers were holding hands and seemed in much better spirits than they'd been in when they arrived for work that morning. They spoke cheerfully as they passed me.

"Are you waiting for someone?" Darla asked as she reached my side.

"My mom. She's picking me up today because I'm delivering a fruit basket to someone in the hospital."

"I hope none of your relatives are ill," she said kindly.

"No. In fact, I barely know the person I'm going to see, but he doesn't have many visitors." I told her how I'd met him and how my family was also babysitting his cat.

"That's very kind of you." Darla smiled and touched my arm. I felt embarrassed, as though I'd been trawling for compliments. "You know, you've been quite helpful, really. I noticed that you took some initiative today in fetching beverages for Mr. Bruno and Mr. Dayton. If things continue to go well, I'll be glad to have you work with us again next summer."

I thanked her, feeling pleased and kind of proud.

"Well, I'd best be off. My husband will start dinner if I'm not home soon, and he's not nearly the cook he fancies himself."

"I suppose you're always the last one to leave so you can lock up," I said.

"Oh, goodness no. There are lots of nights when one or more of the staff will stay and work late, rather than stop in the middle of something."

"But," I hesitated, not sure how to ask what I wanted to know, "the robbery that everyone's talking about. What makes the police think it was Mrs. Thompson if any of the staff here could have stayed late?"

"It so happens that everyone left at five that night, and Marion was the last one out." Darla smiled. She seemed a bit amused by my comment. "But she always locked the conference room before she left anyway. She was very conscientious about security. So, even if someone had been left in the building, they wouldn't have been able to get into the conference room."

She said goodbye then and hurried off to her car. I stood there for a few more minutes and was just wondering if Mom had forgotten about picking me up when she pulled up.

"Sorry I'm late, dear," she said as I slid into the seat beside her. "I forgot something and I had to run back to the house to get it."

"It's okay," I said. "I was talking to my boss anyway. She just left a couple of minutes ago. What'd you forget anyway, the fruit basket?"

"No ... this!" She pulled an envelope out from under the sun visor and passed it to me. For a second I assumed it was from my friend Jane, who moved away earlier this year, but it wasn't.

"It's from Greg!" I squealed. I slid a nail under the corner of a flap and pulled down along the side, open-

ing one end. The letter was two full pages long, and I
sank back against the seat and started to read.

Dear Shelby,

*I was reading this afternoon and a passage
in the book made me stop and think of you.
It wasn't romantic or even about relation-
ships — in fact, it was about a bird taking
flight, how it soared higher and higher
until it almost seemed to disappear against
the sky. I guess you can picture that, though
that's not the point of my letter.*

*What is the point? I guess it's that these
few words brought you to mind. Something
similar happens every day, often more than
once. I'll hear something, or read something (like today) or see something (one day
it was a bottle of applesauce when Dad and
I were at the grocery store — remember the
applesauce you threw all over the place trying to impress me one night?) and you're
there, so close in my head it's like I could
almost touch you. You're in everything
around me, because you're in my heart.*

*Remember once when you asked me
something about my mom, and I didn't*

want to talk about it? I couldn't quite explain back then why that was, babe. I felt bad, because I knew you thought I was shutting you out. I didn't mean it that way. It was more because I'd made a place, a closed place that was only mine. It was inside me, locked up solid, keeping sacred the memories and feelings. I couldn't let anyone touch those memories because that might have changed them, and they were all I had left.

When my mother died, the world lost some of its shine for me. It was like music had gone flat and butterflies had faded and rain just fell, it didn't wash the earth and leave it smelling good and whole. I stood at her grave and all I could think was how unbelievable it was that I was never going to hear her laugh again. She had this funny laugh, like she was going up and down a sound scale.

I wish you and my mom could have known each other. She was one of those people who knew how to listen — really listen. She loved her family and friends fiercely and she never failed to do little things to let you know she was thinking of you, that she was on your side.

*Sounds like I'm trying to immortal-
ize her — I'm not. She was my mother,
and she's gone and I miss her. That's all.
It seemed like it was time to tell you a bit
about her.*

*Why now? Maybe it's easier to say
some things from a distance. Maybe it's
because I miss you so much. But I think
the truth is that it's because you somehow
got into that locked place — got in without trying, by quietly, gently, sweetly,
being you. The girl I love.*

*I got thinking all these things, and I
thought you should know.*

Always,
Greg

I read it twice, and by the second time tears were
running down my face. Mom turned and looked at me
in alarm.

"Sweetheart, is something wrong?"

"No," I sniffed, "everything's fine. In fact, it's
perfect."

CHAPTER TWENTY-ONE

I managed to bring myself back down to earth when Mom dropped me at the hospital with Mr. Stanley's fruit basket, though it wasn't easy after reading Greg's letter. I was so happy I felt like dancing along the corridors, though I managed to suppress the urge.

That came to an abrupt halt just outside Mr. Stanley's door when I heard a woman's **voice**, clearly choked with emotion.

"I hate this, I just hate it." A pause came then, followed by a deep intake of breath. "If there was *any* other way, *any* option, but there isn't and we have to face the facts. This is the third time, Dad. We just can't keep taking chances; our luck will run out one of these days. I'm too afraid of what could happen the next time."

"There, now, it's not the end of the world," Mr. Stanley said soothingly.

"You're just trying to make it easier on me," she said, sounding almost deflated. "I know it's not what you want."

They exchanged a few more words while I stood there feeling like an eavesdropper, which I guess I was. I was thinking maybe I'd better just leave the fruit basket for him at the nurses' station and go, when a woman emerged from the room.

She walked past me without so much as a sideways glance in my direction. She was short and a little plump, with pale hair and skin. Her face showed the distress I'd heard in the conversation, and she paused partway down the corridor and dabbed at each eye with a Kleenex.

Still a little unsure as to whether or not I should go in, I stepped cautiously around the corner and peeked at Mr. Stanley. His shoulders were a little slumped and his face was expressionless.

"Mr. Stanley?" I said quietly, taking another step. "I brought you some fruit, but if this isn't a good time I'll just leave it and come back tomorrow."

"Don't be silly, child, you just come along in," he said, motioning me inside. He looked the fruit basket over, his eyes growing moist. "You've been awful good to me and I thank you. Why, a person hears this and that about young folk these days, but I never did cotton much to that kind of talk. People don't change, really. I reckon your generation is as good as any that's come along yet, considering there's always got to be some bad seed. And here you are, proof of the good of today's youngsters.

"I guess you overheard my daughter and me talking," he said, switching topics then. "Well, it's not going to get *me* down, nosirree. There's lots worse."

"I only heard the last minute or so," I said quickly, not wanting him to think I'd have stood out there and listened any longer than I actually had. "Your daughter seemed upset, so I thought maybe something was wrong."

"Well, it isn't great, but I'm sure there are pluses, too."

"What isn't great?" I asked. My throat felt all squeezed, and I thought he was going to tell me that there was something wrong with him that was more serious than a broken hip.

"Well now, she's decided — that is, *we've* decided — that I can't be living on my own any longer. This isn't the first time I've taken a bit of a tumble, and she's worried that one of these days I'll fall and not be found right off."

"That would be horrible," I said, shuddering at the thought of him suffering alone.

"I suppose it would," he said, as though it was of small consequence. "In any case, it'll not happen because I'm to be shuffled off to a home."

"Which one?" I asked. There are a few senior citizens' homes in Little River, some better than others.

"Depends where there's a bed first, I guess." He smiled, and the lines around his eyes deepened for a few seconds. He couldn't maintain it, though, and sadness crept back onto his face. "Doesn't make much nevermind, where I go. Long as I have somewhere to lay my head, I'll be fine. Only thing I really mind about it is Ernie."

"Ernie!" I gasped, realizing for the first time that this was going to mean he'd need a permanent home.

"I don't suppose you'd be wanting to keep him on?" he asked.

"Well, I..."

"Wasn't fair of me to ask," he said quickly. "I'll figure something out for the rascal."

"No! Don't do anything until I have a chance to ask my mom," I said. "She's really warming up to Ernie. I think there's a chance she'll say yes."

"I know he's an awful scallywag at times." A low chuckle came from his throat. "Only when he's awake, though. I'll sure miss the little guy."

"Maybe I'd be allowed to bring him to visit, once you get settled in wherever you're going," I suggested.

"No sense jumping the gun, now," he said. "Best to wait until you have an answer from your mother before we get to making plans. Could be that she'll have enough sense to turn him out."

"He's kind of growing on her," I said, almost laughing at the thought of how he'd won her over by breaking something.

"Edrie was like that with animals," he said, his eyes drifting off to a time in the past.

"Was that your wife?" I asked.

"Of forty-two years." He nodded. "She was a good woman. A good wife and mother."

"How long ago did she die?" I asked.

He reached a thin hand for the ever-present cup of water and ice chips on his tray, taking several sips before answering.

"Four years this October. It came sudden like, the end for my Edrie. Liver cancer."

"I'm sorry," I said, feeling awkward. It wasn't that I didn't want him to talk about his late wife, but that I didn't know what to say in reply.

"My biggest regret is that she didn't get her last wish," he said, his voice dropping. "She wanted to die at home, in her own bed, with all the familiar things around her. The doctor told me, though, that to control the pain and keep her comfortable at the end, she had to be in the hospital. I did what he told me, thinking that any suffering I could spare her was best, but I've wondered since whether or not I did the right thing."

"Well, you did it out of love," I said. "So that makes it the right thing, no matter what, don't you think?"

"I never thought of it that way before," he said, and his face seemed to soften a little, like some strain had been taken away.

"And anyway, the forty-two years you were married is what counts the most," I added, thinking of Greg and wondering how long our relationship would last. I know we're just in high school, and maybe we'll even break up eventually, but it's hard to imagine that right now, with everything so perfect between us. Couldn't we be one of the rare couples who end up together right from the start?

That got me curious, and I asked Mr. Stanley if Edrie had been his first love.

"First? Well, now, I guess she was. I called on a few other gals before her, but I don't rightly think I loved any of them, though I nearly fooled myself once or twice. In the end none of that mattered. She was certainly the one that counted."

"How'd you first meet?" I wanted to know.

He sipped more ice water and cleared his throat. "We met back in 1952, at a supper they were holding over at the old Presbyterian Church on Weaver Road. It's gone now — burned down sometime early in the sixties and they never did rebuild it. Most folks could travel by car by then, though that wasn't the case when the church was first erected back around the turn of the century."

I was itching for him to get to the romantic part but knew from experience that you can't rush a story.

"So, anyway, they were holding this here supper and my friend Eddy Hosford and I went. We went mainly for the girls, if you want the whole truth," he chuckled, "though there was always good pie and such at those events. That made it worthwhile in itself, lemon pie that would nearly melt off your tongue.

"Well, one of the girls serving at the supper was Edrie. Edrie Ellen McKibbon, it was back then. I recall saying her name to myself and feeling just grand for the sound of it."

"Did you ask her out the night you met her?" I asked. It seemed as though he meant to skip through some of the story, which made me feel cheated.

"Well, now. I put the big rush on her, won her over right quick. We were crazy about each other pretty much from the get-go and we just knew that we'd marry. It was an understanding, mind you, not an actual engagement. I was in no position to take on a wife and home at that time.

"I went to Ontario for three years then, to apprentice as a smithy, and well, that was rough. We wrote a lot the first year, but by the second year it was down to a letter every two or three weeks. Came a time it looked like it was all over between us. Finally, she wrote and told me she was stepping out with another."

"Were you heartbroken?" I asked, swallowing hard. It was ridiculous to feel sad, since I already knew the story had a happy ending.

"I don't rightly know what I felt. Seems it was more like a letdown than anything else. You see, by then I'd almost forgotten what she looked like, aside from pictures, if you know what I mean. It seemed as though it had all just fizzled out."

"But it hadn't!" I said.

"When I got back here to Little River I'd finished out my training. I set up shop, and one day I saw her going by and I went to the doorway and said hello. We got to talking and I found out it hadn't gotten serious with the other fellow.

"Well, I don't know how these things work, but something just swelled up inside me that day, seeing her and standing close to her like that. I up and asked her right on the spot to marry me, and she said yes without hardly a second's pause. So that was it. We married a few months later and I'd say we were happy, though we had our share of hard times and troubles."

The story made me feel good, but almost a bit scared, too, when I thought about how close they'd come to not getting together. I wondered if something like that could ever happen to me and Greg.

CHAPTER TWENTY-TWO

As I walked toward Betts's place I had a strict talk to myself about getting more focused on the whole robbery thing. I might as well admit that the main reason I'd been allowing myself to get so distracted was that I'd gotten to the place where I felt it was totally hopeless.

A quick mental review of the facts didn't help, but I reminded myself that writing things down has always been helpful to me in the past. I'd made notes at work of anything remotely pertinent, but I hadn't taken the time to sort through everything and do up a written overview of what I knew.

The first thing I did when I got to Betts's place was ask her mom a few questions. She agreed, as Darla had told me, that everyone had left at five on the night of the robbery.

"So, you locked up the main door?" I asked.

"Yes."

"What about when people stay late … how do they lock up?"

"It's the kind of door you can lock either from the inside or with a key from the outside."

"And the conference room door?"

"That one has to be locked with a key," she answered.

"Is there any way someone could have done something to prevent it from actually locking without you realizing it?"

"Absolutely not. The key turned normally. If something had been preventing the bolt from moving into place, I'd have known it."

"Are *both* of those locks changed every few months?"

"Yes. They're always very good quality, too, pick-proof tubular locks."

I wished I hadn't brought up the locks again. All it did was discourage me. I decided to switch topics a little.

"Do you happen to remember who was the last person in the conference room that day?"

"I don't think anyone used the room in the afternoon. I doubt if anyone was in there after lunch, though most or all of us would have gone in to get things out of the fridge at noon. The lunchroom was being painted, so the fridge was in there at the time."

"I saw that in the photos," I said. "And Janine told me the fridge had leaked."

"Yes, the carpet was wet. I called a repairman, but to be honest that was the least of my worries at the time. And I didn't know I was a suspect until a day or two later, when everything started to pile up. But I was naturally very upset and concerned about the loss the company was facing with that program gone."

I sighed. I wasn't getting anywhere.

"Aside from the fridge, the room was exactly as it is now in the pictures," I said. "It's just not telling me anything."

"Well, it's a pretty bare room. A conference table, desk, filing cabinets, and a safe."

"There's a water cooler too," I reminded her.

"Oh, yes, a water cooler." She nodded, looking past me as though she was picturing the room in her mind. "And some plants and a couple of stone sculptures. That's about it."

"The plants aren't there now," I said. "They're in the pictures, but they've been moved. Darla has the fern in her office and Debbie's spider plant is in the reception area."

"Well, thank goodness!" Mrs. Thompson kind of laughed and rolled her eyes. "Those two squabbled about which one should be near the window almost constantly from the moment Debbie brought in her plant. Ridiculous thing to fight over, really."

I closed my eyes and tried to envision the picture I'd studied. "The fern was closest to the window, wasn't it?"

"Oh, yes." She smiled ruefully. "No mistake about *that*. Debbie was forever claiming that the spider plant needed the sun more and that ferns don't like direct sunlight. I think she was right, too, and I think Darla knew it, but you know how it is when you say something and then you don't want to back down. She wouldn't give in and she insisted that the fern keep the spot closer to the window."

"Sometimes people get dug in on silly things," I said. I'd seen it lots over the years and I might as well admit I'd been incredibly stubborn about some pretty dumb things myself a few times. "Anyway, I don't suppose an argument over plants has anything to do with a robbery."

"Do you have *any* ideas?" Mrs. Thompson asked then.

"I'm sorry, I really don't," I admitted reluctantly. "But I've got the weekend to review everything. Maybe something will come to me then."

She looked disappointed. I was getting used to seeing that expression on her face.

"Uh, this is probably nothing," I said, "but what do you know about Dymelle Enterprises?"

"Dymelle ... where are they located?"

"Saint John."

"The name's not familiar to me," she said. "Where did you hear of this company?"

"Someone called from there to speak to Stuart. I just wondered because of the student, uh, Gary Todd, having gone there. I wondered if there was a connection."

"It's probably just a client," she said. "I couldn't tell you the names of half the companies NUTEC does web design and maintenance for."

"Okay, well thanks." I glanced at the notepad where I'd made a list of things to ask. So far I'd learned nothing of value and I was almost out of questions. "You mentioned before that the password to access the stolen program could be figured out."

"Yes, that's right."

"Could anyone figure it out? Or would it take an expert?"

"Oh, no, not just anyone. Of course, at NUTEC any of the software developers could do it."

"Could you?"

"Oh, goodness, no."

"What about Darla, Janine, James, Angi, or Carol?" I asked.

"No, none of them. Only Stuart, Debbie, or Joey."

"Don't you think that sort of clears everyone else?"

"Well, not really." She sighed. "A disreputable buyer could easily have someone break the password."

I sighed too. There was only one thing left to ask. "The safe," I said. "Do you open it with other people in the room?"

"Never," she said, shaking her head to emphasize it. "I'm very careful."

It was the answer I'd been expecting. Mrs. Thompson's diligent and cautious approach to security — normally a commendable thing — was working against her at every turn. If she'd left keys around now and then and opened the safe in the presence of others occasionally, it would at least have shaken the case against her.

I could picture her going to trial and being convicted by her own testimony.

Chapter Twenty-Three

Betts hadn't seemed to be paying any attention while I was talking to her mom, but as soon as Mrs. Thompson left the room she practically grabbed me.

"Shelby, you've *got* to find out who did it. My mother *cannot* go to jail."

"Betts, please," I said, swallowing hard. "You have to believe I'm doing everything I can think of, only it's like there are no clues whatsoever to help me. I've met everyone at NUTEC, looked through the file Mr. Zuloft gave me, and thought until my head hurts. I just don't have anything to go on."

She deflated quickly, sinking onto a chair and putting her head between her hands. "I can't believe this is happening to my family," she said, beginning to cry. "We could lose everything."

I patted her arm, thinking what a useless gesture that was. Here her whole world was falling apart, or at least it seemed that way to her, and all I could do was admit failure. I wished I'd never agreed to get involved because then, no matter what happened, I wouldn't feel like it was my fault.

It took a while for her to quit crying. When she had, I suggested a walk, knowing that walking briskly for a half-hour causes the brain to release some chemical that has a calming affect. Or so my mom told me.

"I might as well," she said sadly. "It won't be long before I won't be able to show my face anywhere in town. Everyone will be whispering behind my back, talking about how it was my mother who robbed her own business and got sent to jail."

"No one will be whispering behind your back," I said soothingly. I knew she was right, though. If her mom was convicted, the gossip would take a long time to die down. "Anyway, I don't think everyone goes to jail on their first conviction."

That reminded me of something that had been lurking in the back of my brain and had almost been buried under other things. I told Betts to hold on, I had to ask her mom something else, and I'd be right back for our walk.

Mrs. Thompson was in the back of the house, sitting in the dark in the sunroom they had recently built just off their living room. It's made of rounded Plexiglas that looks out over their backyard, which showcases a fantastic flower garden. In the night, though, it's almost spooky, especially if there's any wind to make the trees that surround the yard sway against the sky. All the bushes and shrubs that are so lovely in the daylight hunch there like goblins and monsters, with craggy arms reaching out to grab you.

Anywhere else in Little River the street lights would be enough to illuminate the yard a bit more, but their place is on the edge of town, at the end of a dead-end street, and the light just doesn't reach back that far.

Mrs. Thompson seemed almost in a trance, sitting there all alone. I wondered where her husband was and how this was affecting him. Did he have moments of doubt about his wife's innocence? And how would it feel to be on the verge of seeing your whole world turn upside down?

"Excuse me, ma'am," I said as softly as I could, so as not to startle her.

It didn't work. She half jumped from her seat and turned to me. My eyes had adjusted to the dark enough by then to allow me to see that her face was kind of crumpled looking.

She cleared her throat. "Yes?" she asked.

"I'm sorry to bother you, but I just thought of something else I wanted to ask you. Have there been any unresolved problems at NUTEC that you can think of? Anything unusual that's happened lately?"

"Such as?" Mrs. Thompson rubbed her forehead with her fingertips as though she was trying to nudge information loose.

"I don't know, exactly." And I didn't. I felt like I was just floundering all over the place. "Anything where things just seemed amiss."

"There *was* something a bit odd that happened few months ago," Mrs. Thompson said slowly, "though I don't see how it could be related to the robbery. We had a big meeting with some executives from head office. There were a number of us doing presentations — Joey, Debbie, Darla, James, and I. The program designers were demonstrating some new software, Darla was doing project analysis, I was doing a managerial report, and James had done up a financial report with projections for future profits and such, based on our output and potential at the time.

"Anyway, I went first, then Darla, and James was up next. Only, when he went to pass out the copies of his report for them to follow along with, it was missing. We'd all put our presentations in there an hour or so before the meeting, on the desk in the corner by the filing cabinets. It seemed that they were all still there, but when he picked up his stack, it was just a bunch of garble instead of the actual report."

"That's odd," I said.

"Oh, that wasn't the worst of it." She shook her head, remembering. "We looked high and low while the executives sat there waiting, and then James found his report copies."

She drew a deep breath and exhaled slowly. "They were in my briefcase, leaning against the wall under the desk."

"What made him look there?" I asked.

"He happened to notice the case was bulging, even though I'd emptied it when I'd put my presentation out earlier."

"How did they get in there?"

"Well, I suppose someone did it as a joke and then didn't want to admit to it when they realized how much trouble it had caused. We looked like fools in front of the executives. But there was nothing actually taken — especially of value, like the program that was stolen last month."

She reached for a tumbler sitting tidily on a coaster on a nearby. "Why did you want to know that?" she asked after taking a sip.

"I just wondered," I said lamely. It wasn't like the two things were related. What I'd mainly hoped to gain from the question was some idea of office dynamics, but the story she'd told me hadn't even given me that. Mrs. Thompson was probably right. Someone had been pulling a practical joke without stopping to think of the possible ramifications. Naturally, once that person saw what havoc was caused, they wouldn't be eager to claim responsibility.

I was right back where I started.

CHAPTER TWENTY-FOUR

The first thing Betts did when we set out on our walk was apologize for how she'd acted a bit earlier. It wasn't a traditional kind of apology, but then friends have their own language about those things.

"It's been pretty weird here," she said, her eyes downcast.

"Yeah," I said.

"Anyway, what I said earlier…"

"I know," I said.

She flashed me a kind of shaky smile and we just kept walking and never mentioned her borderline attack on me again.

"How are things between you and Derek lately?" I asked when we'd walked in silence for a little while.

"Fair to middlin', I guess," she said.

"*What?*"

"Oh," she smiled, a real one this time. "That's an expression my dad uses a lot."

"I never noticed." Truth is, her dad is kind of shy, so the conversations I've had with him have been pretty limited.

"It means so-so."

"Oh." Old people sure say strange things. And they complain about us!

"We're going out tomorrow," she went on. "Me and Derek, that is."

I started to say "Derek and I" automatically, but stopped myself in time. My folks have this annoying habit of always correcting every little grammatical mistake I make. I never thought it would get to this point, but I notice myself automatically doing it in my head when someone else says something wrong.

"Where're you guys going?" I asked instead.

"Probably the theatre. There's not much else to do, especially with the Scream Machine being closed."

She was right. The most popular spot for teens to hang out in Little River had just been sold, and the new owners had closed it for renovations. I must admit it was more than due for a facelift, but it was still strange not to be able to pop in there for gossip and greasy food. Now there was talk that it was going to be changed from a soda shop into an elegant little diner. If that were true, there'd be one less place for us to go, which didn't leave many options, believe me. No one seems to care very much about whether we have things to do in our free time.

"What show are you seeing?" I asked, drawing my thoughts back to our conversation.

"I dunno. Some stupid action show, most likely. Derek wouldn't agree to go if it was a chick flick."

"I know what you mean," I said. "Greg will go to them with me, but I don't ask anymore, because the last time we went to see a romance I heard his father ask him what he was doing that evening, and he said 'penance.'"

Betts giggled at that but quickly grew serious again.

"I wish I had the same kind of relationship with Derek that you have with Greg," she said wistfully. "You guys get along so great."

"Not always," I admitted, though it's nice to have people think that. "We argue once in a while."

"Yeah, only your definition of an argument might not be the same as mine," she said. "When's the last time you two yelled at each other and said mean things?"

"Well, we don't argue like *that*," I said, "but we don't agree on every little thing, either. Disagreement is disagreement, however you express it."

"We *express* it," she said, "in pretty terrible ways sometimes. It seems that lately, instead of having a good time together, all we do is fight."

"I imagine you're really stressed out these days, with everything that's going on," I pointed out. "Maybe that's affecting your relationship with Derek."

"I don't think it's that," she sighed. "Like I told you before, he never does anything thoughtful or romantic anymore."

"Do you fight about *that*?" I asked.

"Maybe a little," she admitted.

"Well, fighting about it isn't likely to make it better," I commented. "Anyway, when's the last time you did something thoughtful or romantic for him?"

"For *him*?" She sounded truly astonished at the idea. "He's the guy. He's the one who's supposed to do that stuff."

"This is the twenty-first century!" I said. "Things have changed. It all works both ways. Or at least, it *should*."

"So you think I should…" She trailed off, hesitated a few seconds, and then turned to me questioningly. "What exactly are you suggesting?"

"I don't know. I don't know what he likes. I don't even think it really matters *what* it is, so much as the fact that you did something special."

"Well, what kind of stuff do you do for Greg?"

"Well, for example, I dropped a little handmade invitation at Broderick's one night, asking him to come to my place after work. When he got there I had a candlelight picnic set up in the backyard. He liked that a lot. Another time I got his dad to let me in his room when he wasn't home and I left a bouquet of helium balloons that I'd written mushy stuff on tied to his headboard."

Betts seemed impressed with the ideas, but her mood turned sour again pretty quickly. "That works with you two because Greg does things like that for you all the time too. Derek never does."

"Yeah, but someone has to *start* that kind of thing. I'd never have thought up the stuff I planned if it wasn't for the fact that Greg did special things for me first. If you still like Derek enough to try to make it work between you, then you might have to make the first move."

"What if I do something like that and he thinks it's stupid and makes fun of me?"

"I guess if it really matters to you, you'll take that chance." I honestly couldn't see him reacting that way, but I wasn't about to come right out and say so. If I were wrong, I'd never hear the end of it.

"You know what scares me?" Betts said suddenly.

"What?"

"I keep changing my mind."

"About Derek, you mean?"

"Well, Derek right now. But it's been this way with every guy I've ever gone out with." She sighed. "I like them a lot and then later on I don't even *know* if I like them any more."

"How can you not know if you like someone?"

"That's the weird thing. Some days I think I'm still crazy about a guy, and others I couldn't care less if I never saw him again."

"And that scares you?" I was having a bit of trouble following her train of thought.

"Yeah. Because, what if that keeps happening to me later on? What if it happens to me after I'm married?"

"I don't think that's likely," I said, but I didn't know if I really meant it. Betts has always been pretty flighty.

"Why not?" She turned and faced me with a challenging look, like she was daring me to say the wrong thing.

"Because, you're still, uh, young," I said, trying to sound like I had some idea what I was talking about. "So right now you're just finding out what you want, you know, in a guy. And by the time you're old enough to make a big decision like that, you'll have it all sorted out."

"But what if there's one person out there who's meant for me, like a soul mate," she said, "and I never find him because I haven't even figured out my own feelings?"

"You believe in soul mates?" I was surprised about that, but mostly I wanted to avoid answering her question.

"Maybe. Don't you?"

"I don't know. I think there could be more than one person you could love and be happy with, though I can't imagine feeling the way I do about Greg with someone else."

Betts's attention was already drifting, though, and I could tell that she was thinking about what I'd said a few moments earlier and not terribly interested in my comments about Greg.

"Yeah, that's cool," she said politely. "Anyway, I think I'll head back home now. I might think of some things to try with Derek, just to see if it makes any difference."

We said good night and I headed home, weary from a long day and a longer week. I was suddenly very lonesome for Greg, and as soon as I got in the house I called him.

He was glad to hear from me, but the second time he caught me yawning, he laughed and said, "There's something I want you to do for me."

"Okay. What?"

"I want you to say good night and hang up the phone. Then I want you to go to bed, but first, make sure your curtains are open so you can see the sky while you're falling asleep."

"Why?"

"Because in ten minutes, I'm going out on the deck here, and I'm going to look at the moon. This way, we'll be looking at it together."

I said okay, said goodbye, changed, brushed my teeth, and crawled into bed just in time. It felt so peaceful and nice, curled up and looking languidly at the moon, knowing that, many miles away, Greg was looking at it too.

CHAPTER TWENTY-FIVE

The last thought that had crossed my mind before falling asleep the night before was how nice it was going to be to sleep in. It would have been, too, if someone else hadn't had a different plan for the morning.

It started out with a rough tongue rasping the edge of my ear.

"Ernie! Stop it," I hissed.

Ernie didn't stop. I mumbled something unfriendly at him and ducked my head down under the comforter. He took this move as the beginning of a new game, one in which he butted me with his head and walked back and forth across my covered head.

As determined as I was to ignore him and go back to sleep, it wasn't very long before his persistence had me fully awake. I knew it was unlikely that I'd get drowsy again.

"You're a *bad* cat," I muttered, crawling out of bed.

One thing about Ernie, he's pretty resistant to insults. With no sign of rancour, he rubbed his cheeks against my legs and purred loudly.

I focused on my alarm clock and saw that it was just a few minutes past seven. With a groan, I washed up and made my way to the kitchen, while Ernie did his best to trip me — running beside me with his little prance and managing to get in front or too close a half-dozen times on the way down the hall.

"I thought cats were supposed to be graceful," I grumbled. Ernie meowed loudly, pacing in front of his dish. He seemed uninterested in any discussion on his clumsiness.

"I *should* give you beef this morning," I went on, getting a tin of food from the cupboard. "What would you think of that? Oh, I know you like fish the best, but *I* like to sleep in on Saturdays and you don't care about *that*, now, do you?"

Ernie purred and meowed and looked impatient. What he did *not* look was repentant.

I plunked his dish back down after scooping a stinky blob of canned trout dinner in it, and he started gobbling like a furry black piggy.

I washed my hands for a second time and opened

the fridge. Mom had made a big citrus fruit salad, in one of her endless attempts to get Dad to eat healthier. It had chunks of oranges and mandarins and grapefruit. I decided to have some of that, along with yoghurt and a piece of toast, but I changed my mind at the last second and reached for the eggs instead.

I beat an egg into a shallow bowl, added a bit of milk, and dipped a couple of slices of bread into it. Then I dropped them into a sizzling frying pan, added a sprinkle of cinnamon, and felt my mouth start to water at the smell.

Once I'd eaten my French toast, wiped the table, and put my dishes in the sink, I found the grouchiness had pretty well passed. I looked around for Ernie, who had eaten and disappeared in short order.

He was curled up in Dad's leather chair in the living room — the chair he's been told repeatedly not to get into. *Any* other chair, we tell him, and he goes straight to the one he's not allowed in and tries to dig his claws into the surface. Luckily it's pretty thick, and so far he hasn't been able to penetrate it, but he still has to learn not to get up there.

I scooped him up and took him to my room. Now that he'd eaten, he was only too happy to flop down and settle in for a nap. I stroked his soft fur while he purred, loudly at first and then softer and softer until he'd sunk into kitty slumber-land, where he doubtless enjoyed dreaming about the next batch of bad things he could do.

I put my face against his velvety side, and in no time, I too had drifted back to sleep.

It was Mom who woke me the next time, although she didn't do it on purpose. She'd started dusting in the entryway and knocked over the umbrella stand. The clatter reached my room and sent Ernie flying to the floor and heading for cover. I knew I'd find him in his now familiar hiding place, behind the toilet in the main bathroom.

Since the ruckus had woken me as well, I figured I might as well give up on sleeping any more. I went and coaxed Ernie from his hiding place and then carried him with me to talk to Mom.

"Did I wake you, dear?" she asked as we came into sight.

"More like you woke him and he woke me," I said, nodding at the cat.

"You woke *me*, too," came Dad's voice behind me.

"Ah, none of you want to be sleeping the day away anyway," Mom said cheerfully.

"I was up earlier," I protested. "I even cooked breakfast and fed Ernie."

"Cooked? Not with real heat?" Dad teased. "You didn't actually turn a burner on!"

"French toast," I said, in the tone you use to tell someone "so there!"

"Boy, that sounds good," he said, looking wistful.

"If you want, I'll make you some. Matter of fact, I'll make you both some," I volunteered, thinking it wouldn't hurt to soften them up a bit before asking if Ernie could stay. It wasn't until I saw Mom's frown that I remembered the fruit salad she'd made for Dad. She's always worrying about his cholesterol and stuff like that.

"French toast sounds grand," Dad said. He clasped his hands together prayerfully and turned to Mom. "Am I allowed, Darlene?"

"Oh, go ahead. You're going to anyway," she said affectionately. "But don't slather it with butter, okay?"

"I promise," he said. "You can even come and supervise."

"You *need* supervision," she said, but she was smiling.

I let Ernie down before we got to the kitchen and started getting things ready to make the French toast. Mom and Dad sat at the table waiting as I cooked, and I waited for an opening. It wasn't long coming.

"Did you find out how Ernie came to have such an unusual name for a cat?" Mom asked.

"Oh! I forgot to ask," I said, making a mental note to do it when I went up to the hospital later on in the day. "I guess Mr. Stanley's news kind of threw me off."

"News?" they asked in unison.

"Yes." Deep breath. "It seems he's not going to be returning to his apartment as he originally expected."

I'd expected an immediate reaction, but neither said a word. They sat and waited for me to explain.

"Uh, see, Mr. Stanley's daughter is afraid something will happen to him, being there alone and all. It seems that he's fallen and broken bones before this one. Anyway, he'll be going into a seniors' home instead. You know, for his own safety and all."

"Well, that's too bad," Dad said. "I think it's hard for a person to give up their independence, though it sounds like it's necessary, all right."

"I don't think it will be so bad," Mom added. "They have activities and things, and he'll have lots of company. And in his case, since he's healthy aside from the brittle bones, he'd be allowed to go out for visits, days or weekends or even longer."

"That would be good," I said, surprised that neither of them had yet seemed to make the connection that Ernie was suddenly without a home to return to in a few weeks.

Naturally, Ernie chose that moment to amble over to the table and jump up.

"Hey!" Dad said. He scooted him off while I hurried over with a washcloth. "I don't think your friend Mr. Stanley overdid it teaching this cat manners."

"You're right," I said quickly. "I think Ernie would be a *whole lot* better behaved if he had a bit more, you know, guidance and stuff."

"Well, I would certainly hope so," Mom said, her eyes smiling. "Since it looks like he'll be staying."

And that was it! No pleading or tears or promises or anything. I was too surprised to say anything, which gave Mom the chance to go on.

"You be sure to let Mr. Stanley know that we'll be happy to have him visit regularly so he can see this scoundrel. I'm thinking that dinners on Sundays when we don't have other commitments would be nice. Unless, of course, he's going to his daughter's or somewhere else."

I was so happy and excited I could hardly wait for the afternoon to come so I could go see Mr. Stanley and tell him the news.

CHAPTER TWENTY-SIX

After the kitchen was cleaned up from breakfast I went and did my room, which I must admit had gotten a bit untidy through the week. I've found it's best to stay a step ahead of Mom when it comes to my room, or she bugs me with comments like "A cow couldn't find her calf in there, Shelby" or "I'd think a young woman your age would take a little more pride in herself than that" or similar remarks.

Fortunately, she doesn't go in there often, but once in a while she'll knock and pop her head in and if it's pretty messy I'm in for it.

Once that was accomplished, there didn't seem to be much to do. Mom had already told me that while I was working through the summer, all I needed to help out with was dishes sometimes, and of course I was to keep my room clean. I guess she thought that since it was summer holidays for me, having the weekends free was only fair. I didn't argue.

With my room organized, I figured it was as good a time as any to compile my scattered notes on the robbery into a more orderly collection. I got out a notebook and started transferring everything that was written in the smaller notepad I'd been carrying around as well as things I'd jotted on various scraps of paper.

The first thing I finished was the staff list, which didn't take long. There hadn't been much to add to the original details Mrs. Thompson had given me, except for a few personality quirks and the fact that the Yaegers had been trying unsuccessfully to have a baby.

Putting the rest of the notes in order was a bit harder, because a lot of the information didn't necessarily fall into any particular category. I ended up with a kind of hodgepodge of scattered things related to the business in general, some of which I crossed off as having no significance.

For example, I'd realized that paying particular attention to any one company that did business with NUTEC was senseless unless there were actual clues to connect it with the robbery. My original suspicions about Dymelle Enterprises hadn't been backed up by any evidence whatsoever. I saw no point in including it in my outline.

When I re-examined the file I'd received from Mrs. Thompson's lawyer, Mr. Zuloft, there seemed to be very little in it that might be helpful. The pictures of the crime scene offered little more than a view of the conference room with the window broken.

Well, that wasn't entirely true, I thought. There were a few other items that were different in the room that day — a couple of plants that had since been moved and the fridge from the lunchroom with the water stain on the floor beside it — but they weren't things that could be related to the robbery.

Or could they?

I stared for a long time at the pictures, willing them to tell me something. I even jotted down notes about the fridge and stuff, along with the other useless things I'd written.

After spending a couple of hours reviewing everything I had and failing to come up with a single idea, I decided I might as well put it all away for the time being. It was pointless to keep staring at the same words, looking at the same pictures, and coming up blank.

Really, the bottom line was that someone had broken the window out *from the inside of a locked room*, and the only person with a key to access the room was Mrs. Thompson. The culprit, I remembered, had gained entry not only to the room but also to the safe, and by her own admission, Mrs. Thompson was the only one who knew the combination.

I'd started into this thing with the idea that there had to be clues that would clear my best friend's mother, but everything kept adding up against her while not one shred of evidence pointed either away from her or toward anyone else.

What if she *was* guilty? The thought came to me, as it had a number of times before, but I knew that I couldn't afford to let myself think along those lines for long. For one thing, it was pretty tempting to just give up. For another, my friend was counting on me, and even if I couldn't actually help, it was important that I stand behind her and her family.

I assembled all the papers into a stack, sat them tidily on top of my desk, and decided not to think about the whole matter again for the rest of the weekend. Sometimes *not* thinking about something can actually help your brain sort it out.

I was about to head out the door to visit Mr. Stanley when the phone rang and Mom called out that it was for me.

"Hello." I tried not to sound too hopeful, though the thought that it might be Greg had already made my stomach start to flutter.

"Great news!"

It was Betts, and her words immediately made me

think there'd been some sort of break in the case against her mother. Maybe the charges had been dropped or new evidence had come to light to clear her mom's name. Maybe I was off the hook!

But she wasn't calling to tell me anything like that.

"You are *so* the best friend ever," she went on. "I did what you said, and it worked, like, amazingly."

"What did you do?" I hadn't quite switched gears enough to follow what she was saying.

"I called Derek's place last night, when I knew he was at work," she said, sounding happy, "and asked if I could come over this morning and surprise him."

"That's it? You just went over there?"

"No, no, no. Of course not. I made him breakfast — little letter pancakes spelling out his name. You know how your mom used to make them for us when we were small."

"Yeah," I said, keeping from laughing. I was pretty sure my mom had made those for us the last time Betts slept over, which was within the last few months. It seemed likely, anyway, since Betts *always* asks her to.

My mom would never say no. She'd whip up a batch of batter and make the letters in the frying pan, carefully forming them by drizzling thinner batter from a spoon into the pan. If you looked at them then they were backwards. Then, when they'd started to cook, she'd add more batter on top to make a normal-shaped pancake, but when you flipped it over, there would be the letter in the middle of it. You could make hearts and other simple shapes, too, but Betts always wanted her name on hers.

"Then his mom called him to get up," she was saying now, "and when he came to the kitchen there we were."

"*We?*"

"The pancakes and me." She giggled. "I guess that sounds silly."

"And how did he like them?" I asked, enjoying the enthusiasm and cheerfulness in her voice. It was a nice change from everything else that was going on in her life.

"He thought they were *great!*" she practically yelled. "I didn't know how to make them like your mom does, with, you know, actual ingredients like flour and stuff, but I took a box of mix and they were pretty good."

"Well, good. I'm really glad," I said, meaning it.

"I *know!* And you know what? I think things might just work out with us after all. He was all surprised and speechless at first, but then he got kind of emotional once it sunk in. It was like he couldn't quite believe I'd gone and done something special for him that way, and when I was leaving he held onto me real hard for a minute and said it was the best breakfast he ever had, which I doubt, and told me he *can't wait* to see me tonight."

"That is awesome, Betts," I said. "And you watch and see if he doesn't think up something for you next."

"I don't even care, though it would be nice," she said. "It felt so good to do that for him. It was like it made *me* like *him* more again too. Weird, huh?"

I told her that I thought it made perfect sense, because I knew how I felt whenever I did something for someone else.

That reminded me that I had good news to share with Mr. Stanley, and as soon as Betts and I finished talking, I headed out for the hospital.

CHAPTER TWENTY-SEVEN

The smell of food lingered in the corridors of the hospital, so I knew that lunch had been served recently. When I reached Mr. Stanley's room I was pleased to see that most of the dishes on his tray were empty.

"They serve something good for a change?" I asked, plunking into the visitor's chair near his bed.

"Soup. Chicken vegetable with soda crackers. The crackers were in a cellophane wrap that I could hardly get open and there were only two of them anyway, so I nearly gave up. I got them, though." He smiled proudly. "And I had a chicken salad sandwich with it."

A dish of Jello wobbled as he adjusted himself to get more comfortable. It was the only thing he'd left untouched.

"Well, I'm glad you're eating better," I said.

"It's not so bad now that I can order my own food. A person gets on to what's passable after a few days here." He leaned forward and added in a hushed voice, "If you ever find yourself trapped in this here place, don't eat the potatoes."

"I'll remember," I promised.

"Well, now, I guess you've asked your folks about keeping Ernie," he said.

"Actually, I didn't have to ask," I said proudly. "When I explained things to them, they just offered right off. They've gotten pretty fond of him."

"Be hard not to," he said huskily. He cleared his throat.

"My mom was wondering how he came to be called Ernie. It's not a typical name for a cat."

"I don't suppose it is," he agreed. "Well, now, would you believe he's named for five Ernies?"

"*Five?*"

"That's right. You see, my littlest granddaughter had first suggested the name, from the character on *Sesame Street*. You know the one with Bert?"

"Sure," I said.

"Well, after she put the name into my head, I got pondering on it. I wasn't sure if it was the right name for the little fellow. Then I got thinking of how so many children had loved watching Ernie Coombs over the years. You know who he is?"

"Mr. Dressup," I said, thinking of the many hours I'd spent enthralled with the show when I was a little kid.

"That's right. So, there was a good connection with the name and children. That's important, you know. But that wasn't all. You see, once I got thinking of the name, I realized there were a couple of other Ernies that I admire a good deal. One was the Blue Jays catcher from back in the eighties, Ernie Whitt. I don't suppose you've heard of him."

"No," I admitted.

"And the fourth was Ernest Hemingway, one of my favourite authors. Have you read anything of his?"

"Just *The Old Man and the Sea*. We took it in school."

"Mmmm. He won the Pulitzer in 1953 for that one. Great book, though I don't know that the practice of teaching it in high school is the best idea. Seems to me a person should know a bit more about life before they can really appreciate most of Hemingway's work." He paused to take a sip of the ice water that was always nearby.

"Something you might be interested in knowing about Hemingway is that he was a real cat lover. In fact, the Ernest Hemingway Home and Museum in Key West houses about sixty cats, and some of them are direct descendents from the cats Hemingway had."

"Wow! That's pretty cool."

"It is, isn't it? And that makes it extra fitting that Ernie is named after him, for one."

"But that's only four," I pointed out. "Didn't you say there were five?"

"Ah, yes. That was the clincher. You see, right at that time it happened that I was reading a collection of short stories, and one of them was called 'A Child's Christmas in Wales' by Dylan Thomas. Anyway, there's an Ernie mentioned in that story. Now, it's not a significant character and he only appears in one line, but the name jumped out at me."

"Because it was a fifth Ernie?" I asked.

"Well, partly, but partly because his full name was Ernie Jenkins. Don't you think that sounds like a perfect name for a cat — Ernie Jenkins?"

I agreed that it did indeed.

"So, that's the whole story. Will you be able to remember it to tell your mother?"

"I think so. But you can tell it to her again sometime, because once you're in your new place my folks would like you to come over once in a while to visit Ernie."

Mr. Stanley didn't say anything for a minute and I thought perhaps he was uncomfortable with the invitation — my parents being strangers to him and all. But then I saw that it wasn't discomfort but emotion that had quieted him.

"You tell your folks that I'd be honoured," he said when he finally spoke. It was in a kind of choked voice, but I acted like I didn't notice.

"How's the book I brought for you holding out?" I asked.

"I'm nearly through," he said, regaining his composure. "I find I tire easily these days, so I can't concentrate like I used to when I'm reading. It's a wonderful book, though. Maybe you'll read it sometime."

"I will," I said. "It's not due back at the library for a few weeks yet, so I'll read it before I take it back."

"You're an awfully good girl," he said, out of the blue.

The compliment surprised and kind of embarrassed me, the way he'd just blurted it out like that and all. I didn't know quite what to say back, so I just smiled. I felt kind of the way you do when you're small and some adult starts saying how cute you are or stuff like that while you're standing right there feeling like a moron.

After a moment I asked him if I could get him anything else from the library, and he mentioned a few books and left it to me to choose from the list. I wrote the titles down in my little notebook, where I'd already jotted down details about the naming of Ernie.

A man came in then and took out the lunch tray. Mr. Stanley snatched his water cup from it just in time to keep it from disappearing with the Jello.

"Can't go any time at all without a sip of water," he told me. "The air in here is terrible dry."

I'd noticed that already, having had to put lip balm

on a few times after even a short visit in there. I wondered what made hospital air like that.

"The girls come around every morning and again before bed to fill this jug up with ice water," he said, pointing to a small plastic pitcher. It had a lid that I think doubled as a drinking cup if you wanted to use it. "It's dandy — cold and refreshing through most of the day. Doesn't get warm until late afternoon."

"I'm sure they'd bring you a fresh jug then, too, if you asked," I said.

"Oh, they would, they would all right. Very good nurses and such working here. But they've got so much to do, lots more important than that. No, I wouldn't bother them for that." He looked mildly alarmed, as though he was worried I'd think he was complaining when he hadn't meant to. "It's fine as it is. Just fine."

"Well, there's no reason I can't refill it, is there?" I asked. I'd visited Betts in the hospital a couple of years ago when she'd had her appendix out and I remembered that there was a little room where patients could get a few basic things for themselves.

"Why, now, I suppose you could." He looked pleased. "That would be lovely. I don't know where the machine is, I'm afraid."

"I'll find it, don't worry." I picked up the pitcher and wandered down the hall and around the corner. There, a nurse pointed me in the right direction, and in no time I'd refilled it with water and lots of ice and taken it back to his room.

Mr. Stanley was thankful, as always. It's nice how something that small and simple can make a difference. It got me to thinking that maybe, once he was out of here, I'd look into volunteering at the hospital. I couldn't come up every day, especially when school was back in, but it wouldn't be too much to give an hour once or twice a week.

I was on my way home, thinking about the whole volunteer thing and how I could fetch ice water and read to folks or whatever was needed, when something shifted in my head. It was one of those quick thoughts that can nearly go right by if you don't catch it and take a closer look.

I came to a dead stop right there on the sidewalk as an idea formed and took hold. The clues I'd thought didn't exist had been there all along, right under my nose — hiding in plain sight. I just hadn't realized what they were trying to tell me! When the full meaning hit me, I nearly jumped and hollered.

It was so simple! Why hadn't I realized it before?

CHAPTER TWENTY-EIGHT

Over the rest of the weekend I checked and double-checked my theory. Everything fell into place, piece by piece, and finally, early Sunday evening, I made a phone call.

"Would Officer Doucet happen to be working?" I asked nervously, hoping I could convince him to go along with my plan.

"He's out on a call right now. Can I give him a message?"

I told her my name and phone number and asked her to please tell him that it was very important. She said she would, but she sounded like someone who hears that a lot and isn't particularly influenced by it. I suppose if you work in law enforcement, your idea of important would probably be a real honest-to-goodness emergency.

It was 10:05 when he called back, and I'd nearly paced a hole in the floor. Thank goodness Mom and Dad were in the living room watching some nature show on television or they'd have thought I was going over the edge.

"You left me a message?" Officer Doucet asked.

I told him that I was certain that Mrs. Thompson was innocent and that I believed I could prove it, if he would give me a chance.

"The problem is, the truth is going to be hard to prove. I'm afraid even laying out the whole scenario won't be enough to get a confession," I told him. Then I explained my plan and what I wanted him to do.

"I know it's asking a lot," I said, finishing up in a rush, afraid he was going to stop me and tell me to forget it any second. "But to even have a chance to succeed, I need you there."

There was a pause, and I could almost hear him weighing my ideas and pleas against his better judgement. Even though I'd laid it all out, I knew everything I'd told him was circumstantial.

"And, uh, you feel you need me there for...?"

"Well, maybe just to witness the confession, if there is one." I wasn't 100 percent sure about what I was asking him myself. I guess I had an idea that he might be able to get an admission that I couldn't, what with his police training and everything. "I thought maybe you could jump in and, you know, put some pressure on or something, help things along. Whatever you can do."

"You seem very sure of your theory," he said. He didn't sound convinced.

"I'm as sure as I *can* be," I admitted. "And you *did* tell me that if I came to you with something that might help clear Mrs. Thompson, you'd listen and really consider what I had. That's all I'm asking. One shot, to help an innocent woman."

"I don't actually start work until six tomorrow evening," he said. "I'd have to come in early."

I held my breath. I wanted to beg but something made me just stay quiet and wait.

"Okay, what time?"

I felt everything inside me kind of sag with relief as we made arrangements. At least I had a shot this way. Without him there, I felt my chances were practically nil.

I called Mrs. Thompson then and told her simply that I needed her to trust me and come to NUTEC the next afternoon. She agreed without asking any questions, though I could hear in her voice that she would have liked to.

Then I tried to sleep.

Monday morning found me nervous and kind of scared. Ernie seemed to think it was a superb time to make a thorough nuisance of himself. He yowled and meowed and head-butted me and just generally went on ridiculously while I ate a fruit cup and toast. I thought maybe ignoring him was the answer to stopping his weird behaviour. I was wrong.

By the time I'd finished breakfast, gotten ready for work, and walked to NUTEC, I was a little calmer. I managed to keep myself from shaking when I walked in and took my place in the spot Janine had designated as my work area the week before.

"The plan was a success," she whispered to me as soon as I landed in my chair.

Her remark startled me for a few seconds and I was wondering how she could possibly have heard anything about what I'd set up for the afternoon.

"With Joey," she clarified, seeing the confused look on my face.

"Oh, what happened?" I was glad for the distraction as I shifted my mind back to her impromptu date last Friday.

"Nothing big, but we had a nice dinner and all, and I think he had a pretty good time. But mostly, I think that for the first time he noticed me as a person and not just a secretary, you know?"

I nodded, happy to know it had gone well.

"So! I wonder if he'll actually ask me out," she said with a sigh.

"I bet he does," I said. I wasn't just encouraging her, either. I really did think Joey liked her. "Look how he always teases and jokes with you, and how he did that program thing without you even asking him or anything. I bet he just didn't want to make a move in case you weren't interested."

"Just like I didn't want to get too obvious with him because I didn't want to make things all awkward and weird between us."

"Right," I said. It was nice to see her happy.

"Well, as soon as I got home I called Jason and dumped him. Not because I'm all sure of myself that Joey is going to ask me out or anything, but because I'm not wasting any more time on losers. I think you're right — I deserve better."

"Definitely!" I agreed, feeling proud of her.

Just then, Joey sauntered through the door, which obviously meant the end of that conversation! He stopped at Janine's desk, smiled and said hello, and chatted with the two of us for a few minutes before heading down the hall to his office. I noticed he had what I think of as a happy walk. You know how someone walks a bit lighter or something when they're happy?

Carol and the Yaegers came through the door next. Stuart and Debbie looked a bit miffed, and it wasn't hard to understand why when Carol spoke.

"You don't need to act like you don't know what I'm talking about," she said before storming down the hall.

"That woman has got some weird ideas," Debbie said. She turned to Stuart. "Did you ever hear anything so crazy in your life?"

"She does get some strange notions," he agreed.

"I wonder what that was about," I commented after they'd gone down the hall.

"With Carol, you don't want to know." Janine shrugged. "She once had a fit because I went to use the copier while she was in the washroom. She said the machine gets used to one person and no one else should use it, or some such foolishness. Like I said, the less attention we pay to her, the better. You can't talk to her at all once she gets an idea in her head."

I found that my attitude toward Carol was quickly getting to be like everyone else's at NUTEC. In spite of her abrasive manner, I couldn't bring myself to actually dislike her. Instead, I felt a kind of tolerant exasperation and rather pitied her.

Janine warned me then that Mondays are usually busy and, as she'd predicted, things got hectic pretty fast. Phone calls and deliveries and correspondence and filing kept the two of us hopping all morning and into the afternoon. We barely had a chance to eat lunch.

And then the door opened and Officer Doucet stepped back a little to allow Mrs. Thompson to walk in first. He walked in behind her.

It was time.

CHAPTER TWENTY-NINE

Officer Doucet took control quickly and efficiently, instructing everyone to assemble in the conference room. Janine was the last to arrive, having stopped briefly to switch the phone over to the answering system and put away some documents.

Once we'd all taken seats he looked slowly around the table and then announced that he had asked us to gather because of a development relating to the recent robbery. I thought that sounded terribly official.

"Miss Belgarden here asked to have an opportunity to present what she believes is new evidence, so I'm going to turn the floor over to her for the next few moments."

I don't know exactly how I expected everyone to take that news, but there was a kind of collective murmur that seemed to fluctuate between disbelief and amusement. It didn't fill me with confidence.

I cleared my throat, which was suddenly dry and tight.

"Uh, thanks," I said. Mrs. Thompson gave me an encouraging smile.

"This is stupid," Carol said, looking around at the others for backup. "She's just a kid."

"I'm going to ask you not to interrupt unnecessarily," Officer Doucet said firmly. "Give Miss Belgarden a chance to speak."

"I'm sure that you'd all like to see Mrs. Thompson cleared," I said. I paused and glanced quickly at each of them. Of course, they all nodded, some slightly and some enthusiastically, but it's not like anyone had a choice.

"There were a few facts about the robbery that seemed to be insurmountable problems," I continued. "One was that the person who gained entry to the conference room had to have a key because the window was broken from the inside. The second was that the safe had been opened and only Mrs. Thompson had the combination.

"However, neither of those 'facts' is true." I paused for effect. Skeptical looks met my announcement. "The person who committed the robbery entered this room from the outside."

"What'd they do, walk through the wall?" Debbie asked. "Was the robber a ghost?" She looked disgusted. "This is a waste of our time, and I have work to do."

"Now, now, let's give her a chance to explain," Darla said. "I, for one, am fascinated to know how someone might have accomplished the impossible."

"But it wasn't impossible at all. It just took a little ingenuity, the right timing, and some special circumstances. Since I wasn't working here at the time of the robbery, it was easier for me to look at everything from a different perspective than those of you who are here all the time. I was able to ask myself if there was anything that didn't quite fit. Was there anything at all that happened at the time that might be considered unusual in any way? And I found a few things."

Mrs. Thompson was leaning forward, listening intently, her face flooded with hope. I saw Angi, seated to her left, reach over and touch her arm ever so slightly, just enough to offer a show of support.

"For one thing, the lunchroom was being redecorated. Every other room here is pretty plain, but suddenly someone decides to change one room." I turned to Mrs. Thompson. "Whose idea was it to do the room over?"

"I believe it was Debbie who first mentioned that it would be nice to have that room perked up a bit."

"Everyone was always saying how drab and unappealing it was to eat in there," Debbie said quickly. "And someone, I forget if it was Marion or Darla, told me I should come up with a colour scheme because I have a flair for decorating."

I nodded, glad to have at least that much confirmed.

"So, the lunchroom wasn't being used and the fridge was placed in the conference room. It was really the only room it could have gone into, and the thief was counting on that."

"In case they got hungry while they were robbing the place?" Angi offered me an inquisitive look over the top of her glasses. Her eyes were twinkling and I knew she was enjoying the whole thing, though whether or not it was because she thought I was making a fool of myself, I couldn't say.

"No, because they needed it here to help with the break-in. You see, when I looked at the pictures of this room from the morning after the theft, there was one of a big water stain on the carpet. The guilty person needed the fridge in here for two reasons. One was to make it look as though the water had leaked from the fridge. The other was to store a large block of ice."

"Ice!" Darla laughed without mirth. "This just gets more and more ridiculous. I'd say that we've all heard enough of this nonsense."

"I don't know why you'd find the idea of the ice ridiculous," I said evenly, "since you're the one who put it there."

"*I put it there?* This is *outrageous.*" She looked around the room, seeking support, her voice becoming shrill. "A kid ... a *kid*, I tell you, coming in here and flinging around wild ideas and accusations."

She turned to face me, anger turning her face red. "And it goes without saying that you don't need to show your face around here again."

"I haven't fired her," Mrs. Thompson said quietly. "And I *am* still in charge here."

"This is slander," Darla said, ignoring her. "You'd better think very hard before you continue with this laughable exhibition."

"I believe that slander is based on lies," I said. The room had fallen so silent it felt almost hollow. "*This* is the truth. Please, just hear me out," I said, looking from face to face. "The water on the carpet the morning after the robbery is very important. Just before the room was locked for the night, the water was taken from the freezer in the form of a block of ice. The desk near the window was moved over to here," I walked to the window and stood where I estimated the desk would have been placed and pointed down.

"If you recall, the water stain was almost exactly where I'm standing, just where it would have dripped if it had started out as ice on the desk, slowly melting as the hours ticked by. The block of ice was arranged or shaped so that it would tip as it melted."

"But why?" James asked.

"Because it was supporting the statue of the wolf. When the ice had melted enough, the weight of the statue sitting on it made it tip — as it must have been designed to do. Once that happened, the statue fell forward. It fell, in fact, against the window, breaking it out from the inside, and allowing entry *from the outside, into a locked room.* You can see that the desk is high enough that the statue would have toppled against the window, but too low for it to have fallen through to the outside.

"Then, it only took a matter of minutes for Darla, who would have been nearby waiting, to climb up and inside, get the disks, get rid of the rest of the ice — probably by tossing it out the window — and put the wolf statue back in place before climbing back out the window and getting away."

"You're crazy," Darla said. Her voice sounded squeezed.

"Hold it," Mrs. Thompson said before I could answer. "Aren't you forgetting that Darla doesn't have the combination to the safe? She *couldn't* have gotten the disks out of there."

"Besides, if someone did get in the way you described, what makes you so sure it was Darla?" Angi added. "Any one of us could have done that."

"That's right!" Darla said. Her eyes flashed at me.

"I know it was Darla because of the fern," I said, "and she *did* have the combination to the safe, also because of the fern."

"What? The *plant?*"

"Yes. Darla had brought a fern in, supposedly to brighten the place up, but it wasn't for that reason at all. The truth is, she had a small camcorder hidden in the bushy fronds, its lens trained on the safe. She set it to record whenever she knew Mrs. Thompson would be opening the safe, and in this way she managed to get the combination. It probably took a while, more than one try for sure, but eventually she had it."

"Preposterous!" Darla said. Her face had gone stiff and pale.

"That's why she kept insisting the fern stay in that spot!" Debbie cried.

"That's exactly why. When you brought in a second plant and moved the fern, she had to put it back because it had been carefully positioned to film the safe. Even though you were absolutely right — the fern shouldn't have been in direct sunlight, while your plant needed it."

"And my spider plant almost died because it didn't get enough sun," Debbie said indignantly. Personally, I thought there were bigger issues to worry about than the well-being of her plant.

"If you think back," I said to Debbie, "maybe you can remember if Darla made any kind of issue over you touching her plant."

"She *did*," Debbie said, wide-eyed now. "She told me I had no business touching her property and went on about it unbelievably. I thought it was just an act she was putting on to make sure I didn't move it again."

"This is insane," Darla said, almost spitting. She pushed her chair back and stood. "I don't have to stay here and listen to any more of this."

"I just can't believe this." Mrs. Thompson sat very still, looking at no one. "Why would she do it?"

"My guess is that it's because she always resented you for taking what she thought of as her job," I said. "You mentioned once that she'd worked here longer than you, and yet when the top job came up, it went to you. I don't suppose that made her happy. The incident a while back, with James's report disappearing into your briefcase — that was most likely her, too, trying to make you look bad."

"Even if any of this was true," Darla snorted, "which it is *not*, there'd be no way to prove it."

"Oh, I think there is," I said, grasping now. I'd hoped she would have caved in to the pressure by that point. "I believe that when the police check they'll find your fingerprints on the bottom of the wolf statue, because you'd have had to lift it from underneath to move it."

Darla laughed, although she couldn't quite hide the fact that she was shaken. "What nonsense," she said, with a fairly decent show of bravado. "Even if my fingerprints were on the bottom of a statue, that wouldn't mean anything. I work here. This has all been most entertaining, but I'm sure we all have better things to do than listen to the ramblings of a teenager with an overactive imagination."

"Well," Officer Doucet said quietly, "it happens that there's more."

You could have heard a pin drop in there, if it wasn't carpeted, that is.

"You see, Miss Belgarden called me with her theory yesterday, and I thought there was enough to it that I did a little investigating of my own today before coming here."

He held up a pink piece of paper, though we couldn't see what was on it. Darla started slightly but pulled herself together as he continued.

"This is a receipt from Little River Rent-Alls," he said, "for an extension ladder rented to one Darla Rhule, the day before the robbery. It was returned the day after."

"So what!" Darla almost spat. "I needed the ladder because there was a bird trapped in my chimney."

Officer Doucet actually smiled at that. "Now, that would be a coincidence. In fact, it would be one of many that happened around the time of the robbery.

Funny thing is, when you get one coincidence after another like that, you can usually get a judge to sign a search warrant."

The colour drained from Darla's face.

"And that's exactly what happened," Officer Doucet said. "My fellow officers conducted a search of your home just a few hours ago, and what do you think they found?"

Darla stood unsteadily. She seemed poised to run but unable to move, like those dreams you have where you're trying so hard to run but everything goes into slow motion and you barely move. She stayed like that while Officer Doucet told us how they'd found the missing software *and* the camcorder complete with the incriminating tape still inside it.

Darla began to fall apart as he spoke. Her lips started to tremble first, and then her whole body shook, like something had chilled her clean through to the bone. When she spoke, it was like something from a movie.

"It should have been *my* job," she said, her voice pathetic and small, like a child's. "I worked hard and I deserved it. Marion *took* it from me."

She looked around then, her eyes pleading, darting from face to face, asking for understanding, but each person in the room, in turn, looked down or away, unable to bear the sad sight.

Officer Doucet stepped forward then, which seemed to finally give her the impetus to move. She turned and ran, racing through the door and down the hall. He caught up with her just outside the main door.

We heard her muffled voice say something, and then she began to cry. Then Joey stood, moved swiftly to the conference room door, and closed it, blocking out the pitiable sound.

CHAPTER THIRTY

I didn't go back to NUTEC, though Mrs. Thompson said I could work there for the rest of the summer if I wanted to. I felt kind of funny being around everyone there after all that had happened. It wasn't that I thought they might treat me differently so much as I felt I'd lied to them all by being there under sort of false pretences.

On top of that, I felt kind of tainted, like I'd been involved in something sordid, even though none of it had been my fault. I'd seen a perfectly normal woman show a side that was so mean and ugly it was hard to believe it was the same person.

I'll tell you something else. Days later I still couldn't get the image of Darla Rhule out of my head. She haunted me, cringing and begging, not for forgiveness but for understanding. I think that was the worst part for me — that she felt so totally justified in what she'd done that she actually expected others to agree with her.

It's hard to imagine someone living the way she must have, with envy and resentment festering and burning in her for years until she allowed it to drive her to such lengths. There she was, working with Mrs. Thompson every day, smiling in her face and all the time hating her so much that she was willing to frame her and see her go to jail.

It might have been easier to understand if she'd done it in desperation, or even for money or prestige, but her reasons were sicker and more twisted than that. She yearned for the job she believed should have been hers, but more than that she wanted to destroy another human being.

Envy.

Resentment.

The charges against Mrs. Thompson were dropped and she returned to work early, since no one else had been trained to fill in for her. Ironically, her employers gave her a raise, probably feeling guilty for not supporting her during the whole mess.

Betts told me she thinks she's going to appreciate her mom more from now on, but I've noticed that this kind of resolution tends to fade pretty fast. Still, I think the whole thing brought them a bit closer together, so some good came from it.

I was at the hospital this afternoon, and I got thinking about how Mr. Stanley had played a role in solving the mystery without even knowing he'd done it. If he hadn't fallen and broken his hip, I'd never have been going there to see him. I wouldn't have been getting him fresh ice water to replace what had melted. That was what set off a chain reaction in my brain and brought me to the place where I realized what the water stain on the carpet really meant.

I also wouldn't have Ernie — the cat named for five other Ernies, who does weird things and almost makes my mom admit she likes him. Almost.

Anyway, here I am, sitting out on my front step, watching the cars go by. It's a warm summer evening with just enough breeze for comfort, but from the smell in the air, a shower isn't far behind. The clouds have been full and threatening for a couple of days now, but they just swell and then seem to shrink back down again.

It's coming, though, a nice warm rain that will wash the earth and give it that sweet scent that reminds me so much of spring. It's a clean, innocent smell, and after what I've seen this summer, I could use it.

I hope it holds off a little longer, though — maybe an hour or two, because by then I'll have seen the car I'm watching for, and Greg will get out of it and come down the walk to where I'm sitting.

I'm guessing that we'll smile at each other like idiots, and then he'll come inside and say hello to my parents and probably be talked into a snack of some sort — and the whole world will be back to normal.

ACKNOWLEDGEMENTS

Writing continues to be a labour of love for me, and I am truly indebted to those whose encouragement and support make it possible. For these and so many other things, I thank:

My husband, partner, and best friend, Brent.

My children, Anthony and Pamela; my parents, Bob and Pauline Russell; my brothers, Danny and Andrew, and their respective partners, Gail and Shelley; and my granddaughter, Emilee. My "other" family: Ron and Phoebe Sherrard, Ron Sherrard and Dr. Kiran Pure, Bruce and Roxanne Mullin, and Karen Sherrard.

Friends: Janet Aube, Jimmy Allain, Karen Arseneault, Karen Donovan, Angie Garofolo, John Hambrook, Sandra Henderson, David Jardine, Alf Lower, Mary Matchett, Johnnye Montgomery, Marsha Skrypuch, Linda Stevens, and Bonnie Thompson.

From the Glenelg Board: Anna MacIntosh, Harold Parlee, Pamela-Beers Sturgeon, Elizabeth Bowes, Joan Jardine, Ray Doucet, Melanie MacAulay, David Saunders, Valerie Krezel, and Heather Dunn.

Individuals who have recently offered assistance, rendered exceptional service, or committed acts of kindness: Pam Despres, Donna Guy, Eldena Gorman, Jim Hennessy, Joy Liddy, Ed Snider, and Molly Trueman.

A few of the reviewers who have clearly connected with stories and characters, and whose comments and criticisms have been a source of help and encouragement: Lisa Doucet, Wendy Kitts, Denise Moore, Carole Morris, Joanne Peters, and twelve-year-old Andrea Nelson.

At The Dundurn Group: Kirk Howard, Publisher, as well as very special thanks to my awesome editor, Barry Jowett (who is also the *real* Ernie's human), the ever-smiling sales and marketing coordinator, Anne Choi, designer extraordinaire, Jennifer Scott, and the fabulous assistant editor, Jennifer Gallant. Working with each of them is a joy.

Teenagers! Hearing from you is the *best* part of writing, and I love getting your letters and emails. So, thanks to: Kayla Church, Erica Cronkhite, Chelsea Derry, Manreet Dhandwar, Aman Dhillon, Marc André d'Italien, Reagan Elly, Kristen Godel, Melanie Gibbs, Chloë Hill, Therese Jodoin, Kaley Kotnik, Raymond LeBlanc, Emily LeMesurier, Cameron Machado,

Shannon Martin, Jackie Mathers, Alexis Muscat, Jessica Neumann, Brooke Palahnuk, Khizer Pervez, Jennifer Pulsifer, Monica Richard, Lisa Svoboda, Fiona To, Meryl Toudjian, Brian Wilcox, and Megan Wrixon.

Regretfully, a recent loss of files prevents me from acknowledging many others who have written, but I truly appreciated hearing from each and every young person who took the time to write.

You are on these pages and they belong to you.